Skipper

Skipper

Part One

RICHARD D. ONDO

iUniverse, Inc.
New York   Bloomington

Skipper
Part One

This is a work of fiction. All of the characters, names, incidents,
organizations, and dialogue in this novel are either the products
of the author's imagination or are used fictitiously.

iUniverse books may be ordered through booksellers or by contacting:

iUniverse
1663 Liberty Drive
Bloomington, IN 47403
www.iuniverse.com
1-800-Authors (1-800-288-4677)

ISBN: 978-1-4401-6972-4 (sc)
ISBN: 978-1-4401-7324-0 (dj)
ISBN: 978-1-4401-6973-1 (ebk)

Printed in the United States of America

iUniverse rev. date: 09/18/2009

Prologue

Casino gambling was a retreat for Richard Stern when he wasn't following a criminal. Frequent trips out of state for business and pleasure put some forward thoughts in his head. He wondered why Ohio never considered casino gambling as a source of tourist dollars. He enjoyed the respite.

Visits to border states started out as a recreational get-a-way. Not for money at first, but it became a serious occupation as time went by. Stern never gambled beyond his means. He learned something from his trips. He learned how to spot terrorists and criminals.

Amateur bounty hunting became serious business after he developed a technique to profile a person just by observation. He never told anyone about the business. When it became a serious source of income, he realized this was a dangerous occupation.

At an early age sports came into Richard Stern's life. He kept physically fit. He used the goodness of exercise to counter act his Achilles heal which was excessive drinking. Too many visits to bars and trips to the local convenience stores for beer and wine softened an otherwise decent person.

The U. S Navy gave him a chance to sail around the world on the USS Enterprise, an aircraft carrier. After that successful service Stern was still looking for adventure. Mimicking the Skipper of the ship, he treated life as if he was still on the high seas.

In later years officiating sports would be a somewhat safer occupation. He could still profile a team, a coach, and players. It was the spectators that gave him trouble.

One could say Stern was a man who wore 'many hats.' First, he had to take some chances in life. The type of work he was doing was risky. That was one of the reasons the FBI came to his rescue.

Gambling for Stern had nothing to do with money. The type of work he chose to do was bounty hunting. He had a single quest in mind with every assignment. In every adventure recovering a reward was the goal.

Playing a dangerous game seemed to be natural for him. Success meant he was alive to tell the story. He was a good competitor. His bank account was a measure of success. Each new profile was a new game.

The FBI used Stern when they found out he could identify criminals. He was like a temporary worker. The heavy drinking was a character flaw and the FBI saw this as a liability. When he started putting agents at risk they had second thoughts. The final straw came when Stern had a relationship with Agent Monica Micovich. FBI Supervisor Cliff Moses decided he couldn't use him any longer.

The FBI knew Stern had a problem, so they didn't shelve him completely. Yes, Stern was a risk taker, a heavy drinker, but he could identify the bad guys. They could call on him for spot duty as an informer.

Possessed by an evil, common to many, the booze affected Stern more than he realized. By ignoring his habitual problem and living with it, he created havoc for those around him. That was the dilemma for everyone associated with Stern.

He was a Gemini, the proverbial June baby. Things always happened in twos for Richard Stern. When looking at the missteps behind him he should have been flat broke and lonely. He is neither. He has money in the bank and a girl friend, Brenda Clark. Stern's adventures read like pages from a Skipper's log book.

Chapter 1
Skipper

One person who values Ohio sports is Richard Stern. While eating lunch, Stern reads the local newspaper about a new recreational park under development. A modern sports facility is being built near Stern's home. The project is to include a golf course, tennis courts, baseball, and softball fields.

Land a mile away from Stern's home was declared a federal cleanup project. Being bulldozed and reclaimed, new soil was being truck in. The two parcels of land were right next to each other, although separated by the Grand River. The recreational development site was on the shore of Lake Erie and it was taking shape.

The old Diamond Alkali Chemical Plant property is being rehabilitated. Transforming the land into a promising recreational playground would take time, but the next generation of outdoor people would have something useful instead of a wasteland.

Would the stigma of a former alkali plant undercut the property's potential? Stern didn't think so. Time has a way of healing or stealing memories. When the golf course is built a new history will be born and the toil of men and women will be forgotten.

Who could have imagined that Painesville Township was about to be the recipient of a second modern sport park? Tiny Fairport Harbor, a village one mile square in area would benefit. With sports parks more competitive events would be coming to Lake County.

Stern's thoughts traveled back in time. Envisioning the land being home to the Erie Indians, this was where they must have had archery competition. Hunting and fishing was their way of life. Father Time and Mother Nature change how the land is used.

Competition ruled the area when Stern was in high school. Stern was a half decent athlete years ago. Lake County, Ohio always had top notch athletes in many sports. Thinking to himself -- *are athletics of today any different from when he was a child?*

Stern's cats had dinner on their mind. He thought the cats provided the perfect listening audience. That's why he spoke to them. The cats paid attention as he replayed yesteryear, but it was food they were after.

"Boots, I was a Skipper. The Harvey Red Raiders and Fairport Harbor Skippers fought it out in football year after year. Fairport couldn't always keep up with the big cities in football. We were too small in number, but we had pride. We got socked when the Diamond Chemical Company closed their doors. You know, Boots, if we had a high school baseball team back then; oh my God. That's one sport our high school should have played back then."

Outside, Stern could hear the neighbor children playing with the dogs. The cats are all ears when they heard the barks of Juneau, the Alaskan Husky, and JJ, the stocky mixed breed. Up to the window leaped Shorts, he knew the bark. Brother Boots stayed near the food. After a quick investigation Shorts rejoined Boots when a piece of turkey hit the floor.

The cats hungrily watched their master as he prepared an E-mail on his laptop computer. They were waiting for a second piece of turkey to fall off the club sandwich he was munching on.

Leaning toward the cats, he reminisced, "Boots, let me tell you something. When I was in sixth grade at St. Anthony's Catholic School, Sister Marie had us on the playground playing baseball, the whole class. She taught us discipline and to be fans of God. The woman was ahead of her time. She liked sports. She was a baseball fan. We had the best teachers and youth teams. Competition was all around us. I was about nine years old at the time. An era of decent sports teams was upon us. The older kids, the light weight Fairport Skippies, they beat a team from New Jersey in football for the national championship and they went on to be high school champs. Thank God sports saved me. I wasn't a genius, but I was competitive."

Richard entertained the cats by flipping them a few strands of turkey. His two little buddies were content for now. The cats didn't mind his trek down memory lane as long as his club sandwich was supplying the food.

"Cats, listen up. Even the Browns won a national title. No, there wasn't a Super Bowl back then, Boots."

The one way conversation paused as Stern started typing on the computer. Stern was busy writing notes and typing and thinking about America's future.

Our state politicians can't see people are leaving to gamble in New York, Pennsylvania, and Canada. They run a state lottery that was supposed to prop up the schools. This lottery can't be working that well if my property taxes keep going up.

Stern wasn't finished. He turned to babble with the cats again. He had first hand knowledge of a state with casino gambling.

"Everybody is gambling. The schools have bingo for big bucks, churches have bingo, and bars have Keno. Some people have always bet on the horses. You know, Boots, somebody is going to build a casino in Ohio one of these days and it better be built in Lake County. I'm going to write to that guy I met in Portland, Oregon. He said he owned the Lewis and Clark Hotel and Casino. It's where I was staying. Franco, Palmino Franco was his name. He said he grew up right next to us in Painesville. He played baseball and football at Harvey High."

With a pen in hand Richard Stern composed a letter.

"I'm going to write a freehand letter. That might get his attention, Boots."

As Richard started composing the letter he wanted to pick on Franco's alma mater. He thought he could connect with Franco's competitive nature.

Dear Mr. Franco,

I met you last year. I'm the guy who lives in Fairport Harbor. We had something in common, our high school teams battled in sports. I think the Fairport Skippers roughed you guys up when you were playing. Don't take it so bad. Well, maybe we had some close games.

I hear change is coming to Painesville, New schools are coming, Mr. Franco. Painesville Harvey is getting a new high school. Maybe you should come see for yourself. This area isn't recession proof, but the climate is right for a casino. Because of the economic downturn in Ohio, this could be a diamond in the rough. Just thought you'd like to know that.

I'm an old Fairport Skipper. Once a Skipper always a Skipper you know. It's just like being a United State Marine. Once you're a marine you're always a marine.

If you still enjoy sports, this is the place to be. Get off your Oregon butt and fly back to Ohio. Maybe you'll see for yourself. This area is ripe for a casino.

Something else, Mr. Franco, you might find this interesting. Baseball, softball, and soccer tournaments are becoming big business around here. The timing couldn't be much better to build a hotel and casino in this area.

Cleveland politics are a shamble. I think you'd find the Ohio governor could be ready to support a casino and I believe the Lake County Commissioners would go to bat for you.

Now that everyone thinks the sky is falling, the time is right.

By the way I sent a letter to the Ohio governor a year or two ago stressing the need to open Ohio to casino gambling. I think all the politicians are starting to wise up. He's changing

his political tune. Ohio will take almost any business if it brings in some revenue.

I hope this letter doesn't end in the trashcan. Please come out here. Visit Painesville, it's becoming the best location in the nation. Do you remember that phrase?

Yours eyes and ears in Northeast Ohio,

Richard Stern
Fairport Harbor, Ohio

The letter went out the next day.

Mr. Stern was a jack of many trades. Stern, the photographer and sports writer, wasn't satisfied with just taking pictures or writing articles for magazines. Although he mostly wrote articles about sports, he had another interest - studying details about criminals. He researched their habits and tracked criminals using the FBI's most wanted list as a source of information.

After years of studying criminal activity he became quite sensitive to behavior patterns. This is how he got started in the criminal identification business. He honed the skill to the point of becoming a self-taught bounty hunter. As he advanced he became embroiled in political and criminal investigation. The amateur bounty hunter turned FBI informer and earned some serious reward money.

The dangerous occupation had some pitfalls. Stern fell in them. He damaged his relationship with the FBI, but the FBI didn't leave him altogether.

The biggest mistake occurred with Agent Monica Micovich. Although it seemed like his fugitive hunting brought in criminals, he put agents at risk. His escape acts were aided by heroic acts. Micovich came to his rescue more than once. If she didn't he likely would have been finished.

She can attest to the danger of being attracted to him. She carries his child, the result of a careless act. Her career was stained by the one night stand. Tormented for a while, she regained self-respect. Maybe marrying Mr. Stern might have made life easier for the beautiful agent, but she was much younger than Mr. Stern.

When Stern worked for the Fairport Harbor Port Authority, he came face to face with criminals at the small boat ramp on Lake Erie. That chance meeting gave him a greater impetus to continue as an amateur bounty hunter. His sixth sense or his ability to correctly identify fugitives was the reason he got involved with the FBI. Actually, it was the FBI that enlisted Stern to be an informer. FBI and Stern didn't mesh very well all the time. Some tense moments created much anxiety.

While the FBI was a benefactor of Stern's adventures, Monica Micovich found it necessary to be Stern's lady luck. The first time she saved him from almost certain death was at a truck stop near Syracuse, New York.

The thirty-something agent got close to him. Even Monica's partner, Agent Paula Gavalia, couldn't help, but see a growing attraction. Paula held her tongue. Maybe Monica was becoming enchanted because she really wanted a father for her child. Monica searched for a decent stepfather for baby Michael. Her journey would end in a crazy way.

Paula held the secret. Few knew who the real father was. Monica never said anything and Stern never realized he caused her pregnancy.

That one-night relationship was a terrible embarrassment. Her unintended pregnancy was testament to that fact. It wasn't that she was promiscuous. Call it poor judgment, a victim of circumstances, or just bad timing, she ended up straining her stellar career, something that was very dear to her.

The decision to terminate the responsibility was too great for the Catholic woman. Father Pete's words helped her make the right choice. She battled through the temptation.

FBI Supervisor Cliff Moses, as he has done so many times with all his team members, helped save Monica's career by restoring her confidence.

Moses trusted his agents. They were often times on their own which were one reason he kept the antacid tablets handy. His two most notable wonder boys, Agent Bill Wright and Ron Roman, were his most capable men. They were the agents to cause Cliff Moses the most excitement.

Along the way Monica and her partner Agent Paula Gavalia learned some valuable lessons from Wright and Roman. Some had to do with work, some didn't. Monica would get jilted by Agent Wright. By becoming too close to Agent Wright, Monica learned a heartbreaking lesson from the ladies man.

Stern had his eyes set on a new business, a sports bar. One problem for Stern, a major concern in his life, was his excessive drinking.

Chapter 2
Mr. Stern's World

Richard Stern's armor in the early stages of life was desire. Like many boys from Fairport Harbor, Ohio, he yearned to be a super athlete. While not the sharpest pencil in the box, he had decent physical attributes. Before he was ten years old, family members, neighbors, and older children marveled at his dexterity and stamina. The quality physical gifts were offset by his exposure to tainted influences which would create a life full of train wrecks.

History can often enlighten mankind. Young Stern had plenty to learn. The value of historic event, both good and bad, provided the bridge to adulthood.

After WW II the baby boom created a wave of prosperity. Using the invention of the TV as a stepping stone, many movie stars emerged. Hollywood didn't squander the creation of the TV. With this new invention the hype grew in the 1950's and 60's, and they produced solid family programs. Hollywood superstars grew their fame and fortune. Movies, game shows, and soap operas' pinned the public to the TV much like the computer of today. Baseball was king and football grew to compete as the American pastime sport. Richard Stern watched a transition of American society from listeners to TV viewers.

Through the middle 60's and into the early 70's the Viet Nam war raged, race riots percolated, and musicians and musical groups popped up one after another. Societal revolution changed America. Mr. Stern witnessed the revolution in music and the dawning of recreational drugs in society. Drug use was another assault on the youth of America. Wine, beer, and whiskey were somewhat condoned as being normal experimentation.

In sports showmanship rather than sportsmanship was starting to taint the atmosphere of the games. Demonstrations on the field during the Olympics started the ball rolling. The game wasn't replayed over and over yet. Teams had to live by the umpire and referee's decision.

Through all this societal evolution Stern waged a multitude of battles from tyke to adult. Smoking cigarettes was a common practice for many adults, but he wasn't completely sold on that nasty habit. His enemy was alcohol, which would run his life. While he didn't want to believe he was an alcoholic, he had all the symptoms.

His friend and neighbor, Dave Skytta, mentioned places where help could be found. Local AA clubs and rehab clinics were the best spots. Perhaps the best source of help Richard would get came from Sunday mass. Father Pete spoke on a variety of issues. In his sermons he would offer words that provided spiritual help. The Catholic priest didn't know Stern was living a double and sometimes triple life as a bounty hunter and FBI informer. He did know that Stern was an alcoholic.

As Stern aged, the ability to hide the truth about alcoholism slid. His undercover world remained a tightly held secret. Even his girlfriend, Brenda Clark, didn't know much about his past. She thought he ran a photography business. Stern wasn't broadcasting the fact that he ruffled a few feathers of some high value criminals that the FBI arrested.

Following through with action was Stern's problem. He just found excuses to deny the truth. However, one day he got the kick in the pants that he needed.

Fairport Harbor's baseball manager's words rang with wisdom. The manager didn't beat around the bush when he identified the problem with the vocal fan.

Mike Mohner said, "Stern, get some help if you have a drinking problem. We don't want you coming to our games as a liquored up spectator. Don't come here if you've been drinking; stay home. Our kids want solid fans in the bleachers."

It was this messages that pierced a hole in his unwilling mind. Much work had to be done to accomplish the task. Missions, battles, and a few journeys were still in the cards. Richard Stern had to wage more war before this tongue lashing would completely sink in.

Stern knew the steps he had to take in order to feel better. The number of trips to rehab clinics could be counted on one hand, but he was running out of fingers. A fifth trip was in the works. Stern didn't go. He decided to do things his own way.

Richard Stern's girlfriend, Mrs. Clark, worked for the Lake County Commissioners. She wasn't entirely committed to Stern. In fact they both played like roving linebackers. Their arrangement was similar to a football team's defensive alignment. They prevented marriage and preserved the right to cheat on each other. Stern was more committed than Brenda Clark.

One day Brenda went over to Stern house after hearing of a composition he put together early in the morning. A speech he prepared for the Better Business Club was in need of someone to offer their opinion. Brenda, who was a master at public speaking, listened to his work and his words.

Brenda says and then asks, "Your voice command is good. I like the business plan, but who is going to have the money to open a business like that in Lake County?"

Brenda didn't have time to discuss the speech. She had to be at a meeting by eleven. Stern raced home; he had plenty on his mind. After Brenda left, Stern turned to the house cats with typical words.

"One more job to do and then I deserve a beer!"

Stern finished framing the last two team photos he promised a customer. With the speech contents still on his mind Stern grabbed his coat and drove to Eastlake. Beef O'Brady's, one of his favorite watering holes, would be open by eleven.

As he pulled into the parking lot he's reminded of his own ambitions, owning a sports bar. Stern buys a newspaper from the outdoor stand. With newspaper stashed under his arm he enters the tavern and finds an open stool as Maureen, the barmaid, draws a draft. She slides the brew to Mr. Stern and asks the usual question.

"Are you still looking for a sports bar, Mr. Stern?"

"You bet, Maureen, Laura and John are going to have some competition one of these days."

Beef O'Brady's Friday afternoon lunch crowd was upbeat. A college football game was about to begin.

Opening the newspaper to the classified section Stern's eyeballs popped out. An old tavern is for sale near the construction site where they're building a sports park. This was close to his home. Downing the beer, he was out the door without saying goodbye.

He called Brenda at work. When Richard mentioned his idea about opening a sports bar she went through the roof.

"When are you going to learn? Richard, that's the last thing you should be considering. How do you come up with these hair-brain ideas? I'm definitely against a bar, a tavern, a wine shop, or anything that has to do with booze. You shouldn't be drinking."

Richard says, "You liked the business plan and I have the money for the bar. I can't open a casino yet, but one of these days, you'll see."

Even though she didn't buy into his plan, Richard bought the building and secured a full liquor license. Within four months he was all set to open the doors. Stern's Occasional Sauce House or SOS for short was an instant winner.

The tavern merely complicated Stern's life. Brenda was not a happy camper, but then again she wasn't exactly an angel. They were drifting apart if not in full retreat. She was making new political friends.

Richard got wind of Brenda's extra activity and in a bid to return the decadence he started a romance with one of his employees. Stern and Brenda's lack of respect for each other had the usual consequences. They hurt each other, acting as if each was a voodoo doll. The pins of deceit pierced their hearts until they found common ground when Stern ended up in the hospital from heavy drinking.

Stern could go for quite a while without drinking, but once he started the flood gates were open. He could never put the cap on a bottle of booze.

When the sports club first opened he remained faithful to the business, only having an occasional beer. It didn't last for long. Controlling his drinking problem was like predicting the weather. It was bound to be out of control. Relapse and the hospital were not far away. Stern was always sneaking in a cold beverage even after his hospital stays. This opened the door for more socializing. It was a problem for his bar manager.

The bar manager, Anita DiDomenico, made a plea to Stern.

"Richard, you're drinking more and more each day. I'm concerned as are Carrie and Whitney. Don't take this wrong, but you aren't helping business if you're intoxicated."

Anita's words had little effect. The disease was in full bloom. He was regarded as cool to his drinking buddies, but was losing the respect from his employees and decent paying customers.

After a month Stern was his own doctor, administering maintenance drinks to himself just to function. This went on until his body started to reject the abuse. Brenda stopped in one day in spite of their strained relationship. She saw him as a loving friend and felt guilty because of her socializing. She knew he needed help. Although she wasn't a saint, compassion was her first order of business.

"You need to check into Lake West, Richard. You're sick. I want you to do this. I'll drive you there after I finish work today."

Richard, in a defiant mode tried to reassure Brenda that he was going to get better on his own. This lie was the pattern he used all his life.

"I really do miss you, Brenda. I can handle it. I've got a business to run."

"I'm not going to watch you kill yourself. You ask Anita to run the business. If she can't help full time call Laura Werner. If Laura can run a major operation like Beef O'Brady's, she can run this place. Maybe her son, John, is willing to run this tavern until you get better," said Brenda.

Richard answered instinctively, "Let me think about it."

He knew she was right. He grabbed her hand looking for sympathy.

"You always have the logical answer, Brenda."

Sometimes thoughtful, she was a dynamic communicator. Staying on track and finishing the job are parts of her persona. However, that didn't apply to her love life, although, deep down she wanted him to be close to her. She could live with him if he made the right choices. Her next line of logic was another arrow into his ego.

Brenda says, "Don't you think you should sell the tavern? When you're this close to what has been the problem in your life; well, let's just say this isn't your bag. Richard, you do well when you're sober. I'll help you. You don't have to live like this."

"Brenda, I'll make the right decision. I'm the guy who has to make the next move. Maybe by tomorrow I'll know. I'll meet you tomorrow if you want to patch things up. I'd really feel better if I knew we were going to be together again."

Brenda relented for the time being. Business calls had to be made on behalf of the commissioners. She had to return an important phone call that was beeping on her cell phone. A call was coming from one of her social friends in Columbus.

Stern entered the hospital on his own after telling Anita he would be gone for a few days on business. After checking in over a long weekend, he didn't stay long enough. Checking out after three days, his condition was only stabilized. Without going through the thirty days dry-out period he could almost count on reconvening where he left off.

Brenda received a call from Richard during the stay. She was ecstatic that he was getting help. Days later she learned that he didn't stay in the hospital. She was happy and sad at the same time. At least for now they patched a friendship together. This way she had a chance to keep an eye on him. Unfortunately, she couldn't always be around to watch him and she had trouble avoiding new romances.

Chapter 3
Matrimony Not

Tragedy struck just before Monica finished high school. Her mom and dad almost died together in the car crash. She was guided by her father's last wish. He asked that Monica follow his example. Mr. Micovich was a National Security Agent who traveled extensively. She wished to follow in his foot steps.

Monica Micovich's Catholic upbringing was instrumental in molding a leader.

Like her father she graduated from Lake Catholic High School and went on to St. Leo University in Florida where she stood out as a person above all.

As captain of the high school volleyball team, she was torn between two sports which played at the same time. When allowed, she played soccer as a lightning fast forward and was a perfect setter in volleyball. She picked soccer when a scholarship offer came her way. She was a fierce college soccer player. Adding to her list of attributes, she was bright, articulate, and brave. Her self-defense skills came in handy because of her occupation. She could handle men twice her size.

She didn't date much in school, but was popular just the same. The boys knew her father taught her self-defense techniques which may have been a reason the boys were intimidated. After his passing she became even more accomplished.

She wanted to find a man like her father and this may have been the reason that love passed her by. Mr. Micovich was a bit of a drinker, but had a sterling record in law enforcement.

Monica was shocked by her pregnancy, but her faith held strong. She needed to find someone. Although Richard Stern had some of her father's traits, he wasn't the type of father and husband she envisioned.

Monica did find a handsome, brave man. Their Romeo and Juliet relationship was supposed to be a perfect match between FBI agents. Bill Wright and Monica Micovich's relationship slowly melted away. As Monica grew noticeably pregnant, her change weakened Wright's enthusiasm for his sweetheart. Monogamy wasn't a practice Bill ascribed too. He couldn't contain his incessant desire for women.

They talked about marriage and acted as if married. Truth and honestly was lacking. Although Monica confessed to Bill that he wasn't the father, she hid the truth about who was the real father. Bill, he was still playing the field with no regard for Monica's feelings.

On Sundays Agent Micovich would travel from her home in Willowick to Fairport Harbor to hear the Catholic priest's sermons. Monica trusted the straight talk from Father Pete Mihalic. The spiritual words restored her faith and motivated her. She wanted to move to Fairport Harbor. The little parish, St. Anthony's of Padua, was a guiding light for her. She could hang her troubles on the outstretched arm of Jesus Christ and walk away leaving them there.

Father Pete gave plenty of sermons from the pulpit to reflect upon the bond between husband and wife. He would say that marriage is commitment. Love and honor help to fuse that commitment.

"The sacrament of matrimony is the cement that bonds a relationship. Your Catholic faith will help keep marriages cemented," said the pastor.

Monica could hear his words. It was Father Pete's words that gave her strength to overcome the temptation to override her pregnancy.

The words danced in her head. She understood the meaning. It was Bill that lacked commitment and Monica was full of wishful thinking. The baby was nearing full term making the situation a state of urgency.

She wanted the baby to have a decent father. Bill Wright had many traits that made him qualified. Dashing, brave, and loving were the traits she saw while overlooking his playboy mentality. While she knew Bill was a lady's man, she excused his wandering eyes, wishing and hoping he would settle down. She prayed that Bill would become the foster father.

FBI Supervisor Cliff Moses tried to be sure Monica's role in his department was out of the pressure cooker, although she insisted on working some tough cases. Answering a phone wasn't Monica's idea of being an FBI agent. Because of her persistence and badgering, she was given important work, but mostly, it was low level investigations. When the workload increased she took bigger assignments.

Cliff understood the strengths and weaknesses of his agents, so he felt confident in their abilities. He wanted to make adjustments as Monica's delivery date drew near. His planned vacation was approaching. He postponed the date once already because the department had several hot cases being investigated.

Hot jobs always seem to surface unexpectedly. For his top agents, Agents Bill Wright and Ron Roman, they were teaming in the field on a whopper case involving shipments of weapons. Monica was involved in a political case. It proved to be a difficult investigation. Since she would be taking a leave of absence, he needed to know if her case could be wrapped up. If not, another agent would have to pick up where she left off.

Monica's everyday partner and best friend, Paula Gavalia, started working with Julie Suhadolnik, an agent with a background in chemistry and explosives. Because of her specialty, Julie was called away from time to time to work with the National Security Agency. During these deployments, Moses' female crew was stretched thin.

Moses finally decided to let the clock run out. He would leave the country without changing the date.

He was finishing up some last minute work. Packing items away, anticipating the day he could break free from the hectic schedule.

Supervisor Moses says, "Monica, someday you'll need to learn my job. How about sitting in for me?"

Monica asks, "Do you want me to push a pencil?"

Cliff answers, "No, just sit in my place for a day and make sure you update all of your files before I leave. I'm going to Columbus; I might be back tomorrow. My trip to Europe is getting closer; I'm serious this time. I'm really going to Europe."

Monica replies, "Well, if that's the case, the answering machine will have to do. I'm leaving town, too, Cliff. I'll take a crash course in updating the files. I'm trying to finish up my cases."

Cliff says, "A crash update is good enough. This time I'm really leaving to tour Europe."

Cliff had to keep reminding himself about his vacation. He left Monica in charge as he departed. Monica sat there for an hour. The desk job would have to wait. She needed to follow up on her own case. She picked up the car keys and she raced out the door.

Supervisor Moses always hoped she would take a back seat during the tense moments of an investigation. This was wishful thinking, especially for the conscientious agent. She was a self-starter with a mindset to finish the job.

Although it was obvious the Negro supervisor wasn't her father, in certain instances he acted as if he was. Looking after his agent, he faulted himself for the situation that compromised Monica's career. Moses blamed himself and had a difficult time getting over the mistake.

Since that time Monica Micovich was busy busting crooked politicians and leading the charge for the department. It didn't take her long to regain the department throne as a leading investigator.

During her new role as lead investigator Agent Micovich received logistical assignments that required her to travel. Some of the work was tame. She knew Cliff was trying to reduce her tough assignments. She didn't like it, but relented for the sake of the coming arrival. She was removed from the late night stakeouts with Agent Gavalia, which were tedious and sometimes grueling tasks in some seedy areas.

At times, she carried on as if she wasn't pregnant. Meticulous in her manner, she carried out her assignment exceptionally well, but was slightly slowed by her pregnancy.

While Monica was away, Bill Wright couldn't contain himself. Wright, the playboy, found time to mingle with the opposite sex. After nearly eight months of dating then living with Monica, Wright's heart floundered. His mendacious behavior turned into infidelity.

A nightclub meeting between a young woman and the wolf turned into a galvanizing romp. The night ended with the twenty-one year old college student asking for a date. Bill, noted for one night stands, was pleased by the offer. He didn't refuse. After a late night date and three more encounters at the nightclub the charade ended.

A picture of Wright and the young woman was taken by Monica's friend, who happened to be at the nightclub. She sent the picture by cell phone. It landed on Monica's cell phone. Monica flipped. The picture raised the hair on the cat.

Forlorn by his action, she sank and cried. Her first impulse was to E-mail the two-timer, but she composed. She didn't say anything to Bill. Based on his past history with women, she knew the picture didn't lie. She continued her work, only now, the job turned into a passion. Her heartache was real. The love affair she thought she had with Bill was ruined. The scorn of a woman betrayed was undeniable. It turned Monica into a voracious crime fighter.

Released from the phony bond she thought she had with Bill, Father Pete's warning words echoed in her head.

He said that 'shacking up isn't marriage. There is more to know about a partner.' The pastor's righteous words were on target.

Monica got a temporary release of her anger. Work was the best medicine. Her carefully crafted sting was scheduled to go down. The next day the gloves were off. The Detroit mayor was miffed when she entered the mayor office with pictures of the mayor excepting an envelope from a contractor. Monica setup the operation. The envelope was an FBI plant.

Next on the slate were more politicians. State senators were on the special pay off list that Monica confiscated from a business being investigated for embezzlement. Monica was on a roll. Business was booming at the prosecutors' offices in Michigan, Illinois, and Ohio. During the investigations, Monica made plenty of enemies. The Chicago mob was feeling the heat as she turned the screws on corruption. The mother to be was a crime wrecking machine. She was stepping on the toes of mobster bookies who thought they had immunity because of their ties to the political network. Even the politicians were getting antsy.

The crisis was hurting the book-making operation of the syndicate. Some hand wringing was going on which started a cascade of phone calls between politicians and the syndicate.

After a month away from Northeast Ohio, Monica boarded a plane back to her home town in Willowick. The small Ohio city was only twenty minutes from her office in Cleveland.

She landed at Hopkins International airport. A text message to Bill was deliberately incorrect. She wanted him to wait at the wrong gate. She mentioned having a surprise for him. The occasion was to be a memorable one.

After she landed, Monica sent Bill another message.

"Bill, go to gate C, flight 1107 arriving from O'Hare."

Any chance of matrimony with Bill was finished. What stood out in her mind was a cracked wedding bell and wilted roses. All that remained in her mind was the picture of the hussy and Bill. Monica saved the cell phone picture of Agent Wright in a lip lock with the young beauty. The text message and picture was from a friend with credibility. The friend was a victim of Bill's turpitude.

Monica had no warning for Bill as they saw each other. She went right for the jugular. She held up the cell phone picture for him to see.

Monica asks, "Do you have a new girlfriend, Bill?"

Monica moved her cell phone closer to his face.

Monica says, "I got the picture. Let's see if you get the picture, Bill. You're no different than that other Bill that was in the White House. You both feast on young women." She thrust the cell phone close to his nose.

"Take a good look, Bill. This must be your kissing cousin, right."

The picture told a thousand words. Dancing around the truth wasn't an option for the playboy. He didn't do a two-step around the question.

"Monica, I'm truly sorry. I'm not that strong when it comes to women," admitted Wright.

Monica lashed back. "I'm pregnant. I feel fat, and not available. You're on the hunt. You're a jerk. Go get the young chick. You won't ruin my life. I should've known," cried Monica.

Bill scanned the concourse. People were gazing, some amused, others concerned. Bill was awe struck by Monica's full-court press. Strangers almost wanted to offer help as Bill tried to temper the moment.

"Monica, I'm weak." The tempo quickened. This wasn't an orderly outburst as Monica came to grips with her own misconception of a father and a lover. She dished out heated words.

"Well spoken, jackass, the hussy needs a weak guy like you. We are through, Bill."

Dashed expectations, duped by her partner, she dropped the cell phone in her purse and started walking away. Bill Wright, the weasel, stood at attention almost like a new recruit facing the irate gunny sergeant. In shock, embarrassed, he held out his index finger as if he had a correcting point to make.

"Wait, Monica!"

Her broken heart wasn't completely empty. Although the fire was out with Bill, she felt the kick of another body. Again the kick was from within her; the baby was urging closure. She turned to Bill with last words.

"Wait for you, no, Bill. Someone else is signaling me. I have someone decent inside of me. You have the hussy; leave us alone."

Another contraction almost ended her conversation. She refused to signal her labor pain.

"One of these days, you'll regret being a two-timer. I'll take a cab! I'm strong!"

True, Monica was strong, but the end was painful. Monica walked to the ladies room and doused her face with water. The next contraction was stronger. She called Paula with the news. Paula listened.

"Bill's been cheating on me. Paula, he can have her, we're through, but I think something is more important right now." She paused and clenched the phone.

"Paula, I'm in labor!" Monica had to leave the full story for another time.

Another contraction was followed by a pause.

"He's coming, Paula, the baby, he coming! I'm going to the hospital; Lake West, but it might be Euclid General, maybe Cleveland Metro."

Fearing the timing was out of sync along with being emotionally hurt and in labor; she ran to the luggage pickup station trying to remain calm. Her baggage was in sight. Monica grabbed her baggage as if she knew she had ample time.

Outside, cabs were lined up. She wasted no time grabbing the lead cab.

The cabby loaded her bags. As she jumped in the cab, he asked where she wanted to go.

Monica responds in a matter of fact, nonchalant way, "Let's try for Lake West Hospital in Willoughby; they know me there. I'm in labor. I'm going to have a baby."

"What?" The driver asked."

Monica was determined to take care of herself. She looked at his cabbie ID and winked at him in the rearview mirror.

The cabby swung his head around; the astonished look on his face was telling. Monica motioned to him with a flick of her hand.

"Go! Move it, we have time. You're going to remember this moment," says Monica.

The cabbie responded, "You can say that again, momma; I'm gonna get you there; don't worry."

Monica says, "I have a hundred bucks, plus a twenty just for you, please drive safely."

Jackson, the cabbie, heard the magic words, but he was already motivated.

"Oh, baby. Put your seatbelt on. Jackson's got wings, and I'm flying, momma."

"Jackson, just drive safely."

The drive was swift. All the while Monica counted the seconds between contractions.

She peeled off a hundred dollar bill and a twenty as they pulled up to the emergency entrance at Lake West Hospital in Willoughby.

She studied his ID on the visor. "Is that your name, Mr. Michael Jackson?" asked Monica.

"Michael Jackson, momma, but I can't sing."

She answers, "But you sure can drive! Keep the extra Jackson, Michael Jackson."

"Here you go," says Monica as she slaps the bills in his hand.

Monica was out the door. Together they moved to unload her baggage. As they entered the lobby she thanked the cabby.

Calmly, Monica walked up to the receptionist. Luggage and all at her side, Monica greeted the young woman as if Cinderella's hour had sounded.

She says, "I'm in labor, and he's coming fast!"

Paula called Cliff Moses with the news.

"Cliff, Monica's in labor. I'm not sure which hospital she'll be at, but she said Lake West was her first choice. But then she added Euclid General or maybe Metro. That's Monica alright. She always has a plan B and a plan C."

Excitedly expressing the news, Paula wanted Cliff to know about the breakup.

"Something else I better tell you. I know you were concerned about Bill and Monica. It's over, according to Monica. It sounds like the mating game is over.

Cliff says, "Thank God."

Paula answers, "I'll go to Lake West first. Stay by the phone, boss. I'll find out more and call you back."

"Thanks, Paula. I'll be either here or at home waiting for your call."

Chapter 4
Ashamed

Unceremoniously coming into the world is Michael Micovich. The natural birth of Monica Micovich's first child was an emotional battle more than a physical labor. Oh, she suffered through the push, but her thoughts turned to naming the child. It was a struggle for her.

Her partner and best friend Paula Gavelia made it to the right hospital for the delivery. Although Monica wanted the birth to be a private event, she was comforted by Paula during the delivery.

Miss Micovich had strong reservations about naming the father. Some close friends and co-workers knew, but Monica was hesitant about putting a father's name on the birth certificate. This was just one of the difficult judgments Monica needed to make.

"Monica, we hope you name the boy's father. The nurse said you don't want to reveal who the father is. That's your right, but why? This is a beautiful, healthy baby," said Dr. Mack Ivory, the obstetrician. The doctor could see Monica was struggling with an answer.

"Doctor Mack, I can't give you that name." Deeply ashamed, Monica bit her lip. Stubbornly refusing the doctor's inclination, she acted as if she was on the receiving end of an interrogation.

"Monica, a pediatrician sometimes relies on the medical history of the parents to diagnose trouble. This valuable information should be shared with the doctor."

Wrangling with the decision, Monica held her tongue in check. She didn't want Richard Stern's name on the birth certificate. He was twenty years older than she and he was an alcoholic. How could she face the shame? Her miscue was bad enough without plastering his name on a state record and then she would have to look at it.

Alarm bells sounded in her mind, but she knew Richard loved her. The perfect father, he wasn't, she thought. Stern might end up embarrassing them.

The nurse came forward with helpful words. She could see Monica was torn by this decision. Attempting to sooth her struggle, she said, "Don't let this decision wear on you. You don't have to name the father, Monica. It's a mother's right."

The advice of the obstetrician was difficult to swallow at first. Monica tried to explain to the doctor her reasons for keeping the father's name off the birth certificate.

"He's a drunk," said Monica. Her voice cracked in an elevated tone.

She closed her eyes remorsefully reflecting on the episode that tainted her career. She wanted to forget, yet her memory was vivid. When the National Security Agency selected her partner, Agent Gavalia over her, she regarded the move as a slap in the face. She was sidestepped for a highly dangerous operation which she felt was her job to do. Emotionally stunned by the bureau, she left her guard down.

Her mind swept through the past. She was guarding Richard Stern who was a target for assassins, because of his bounty hunting. As they were watching an Indians baseball game on TV at a sport's bar in Cleveland, she acted out of character.

Monica was unaccustomed to drinking. Oh, she did some partying in college, but never excessively. However, this time with Stern ordering the beers she made the mistake of dulling her senses. After a couple beers she was giddy. The combination of events made her weak, almost hypnotized. Richard had a knack for talking in a relaxing voice.

A tinge of recollection hit her square in the memory bank.

"Damn, why did I drink?" She whispered as her mood swung from mother to fuming dragon. She tried to shift the blame.

"It was Richard's fault!" She paused, trying to find someone to blame. She was tearing herself apart. It dawned on her. Maybe the bartender and Mr. Stern were behind the effort to get her drunk.

Although her answer was skewed, she refused to share the blame.

"They were playing a cruel prank. The prank was on me! Stern, the alcoholic, he's the one!" voiced Monica.

As Dr. Ivory and the nurse discussed the clerical issues; he listened and overheard Monica's elevated tone. It was evident she was reflecting on the past and not talking to the baby.

Dr. Ivory moved to her side.

"It's ok, Monica. It's over. You are a mother now. You have a healthy baby boy."

The doctor continued to explain as Monica came to terms with her conscience. Her memory flashed to Father Pete who offered her spiritual guidance. She understood this is a gift from God as she held her baby boy.

Doctor Ivory offered clarifying advice.

"You needn't be ashamed about what happened so long ago. The baby has a father and you can name him, or leave him off the county record. I'm helping you preserve the facts. Record the father's name, Monica; it's the right thing to do. Besides the financial obligation, the medical history of the father can often help in diagnosing allergies and so on."

On the verge of breaking, Monica admits the truth. "Richard Stern, Doctor Mack, the father is Richard Stern."

Monica, ashamed of her salacious act, started to cry. She was still deeply hurt by her own lack of self-control.

"I fell for an old trick. I was very distraught, Doctor Mack. I left my guard down. I'm the one who drank excessively."

As the doctor moved to comfort her, she regained her composure.

It was as if an angel appeared with the missing piece of a puzzle. Hating to be wrong or duped, Monica accepted reality.

In her arms is a beautiful baby boy. He is her son. She finds the birth of a child is a stepping stone to heaven.

"You're the best mistake I ever made. No, you're the best decision I ever made." She cries tears of joy. It is a powerful moment. The epiphany gives the new mother badly needed peace, even though it would not last.

The doctor put his arms around them. Understanding her emotional ebb, he follows up with a guess about the future.

"He'll be a handful, Monica. You're a professional, highly educated, and you're athletic. Who knows? Maybe Michael will be a baseball star."

Chapter 5
Hotel Magnet

*O*rdinarily Brenda Clark is cognizant of influential people who wish to see the county commissioners. Her duty as a task master and preliminary screener is important so that nearly everyone is afforded an opportunity to voice an opinion. Without an appointment it's nearly impossible to meet with the Lake County Commissioners.

Palmino Franco, a hotel and casino entrepreneur, returned to Northeastern Ohio from Portland, Oregon. His Lewis and Clark Hotel by the Williamette River will operate without him while he travels to Painesville, Ohio where he grew up and went to school.

Franco was a high school athlete, a United States Marine, and later a star college baseball player who never lost focus on staying physically fit. As a college baseball relief pitcher; he was a specialist. His work ethic earned him enough recognition to land him a Double AA contract and a shot at Triple AAA ball. The Mud Hens soured on the pitcher after he blew out his arm. He finished college, took a job out West as an assistance manager of the Victory Hotel.

A Sicilian family friend traded money for antiques. With the wealth he bought a controlling interest in the Victory Hotel and he parlayed that investment into the Lewis and Clark Hotel and Casino. Along the way a small Mafia type struggle ensued which eliminated some investors. Even he was a target for extortion. The plot was exposed. Mafia members landed in jail. In the end Franco was the last man standing. The hotel and casino became his.

He learned some valuable lessons during the struggle. Dealing with the criminal elements only promised a courtship with evil. Franco feared negative publicity when it came to casino gambling. To circumvent negativity he became a public liaison.

Carefully linking local sports associations to the hotel and supporting youth programs with casino revenue he nurtured positive opinions of the way he does business. He operated his casino as a family extravaganza. Gambling floors were isolated well away from family entertainment. He succeeded in this way by making friends and keeping problems to a minimum.

The letter from Richard Stern stimulated Palmino Franco's curiosity. A man with an eye for opportunity, Franco returned to Lake County, Ohio. This vacation was an investigation in part and a return to his roots. Accompanying him on the visit was his business attorney Simone Porter, a young woman with a razor sharp memory. Although she had her eye on the much older casino owner, she wasn't a gold digger.

Every now and then Franco thought about owning an eastern bastion entertainment wing. It had been on his mind, but he didn't think it would work well in states that had casino operations already in place. The fact that Ohio, his original home state, didn't have casino gambling intensified his interest.

Upon returning to Northeast Ohio he found the areas around Lake County had transformed into modern towns and cities compared to when he was growing up. On the other hand his view of greater Cleveland was one of disdain. The whole of the city was mired in neglect and stagnation. He thought high taxes and political debauchery were strangling the once magnificent city.

The political climate was changing. A casino in Ohio was definitely a possibility because the economy was limping. Stern's letter indicated a reversal in the way Columbus viewed a casino. Gambling proponents didn't have the votes and the casino issue was voted down twice. Political willpower was motivated by the economic meltdown. The positives did out weight the negatives. A new battle cry was sounding from Columbus.

"The people want a casino built in Ohio," said the top Ohio political figure.

Suddenly, a casino made sense to those standing on the sidelines. Where should we build and who would have the muscle to get the job done right? Some people knew building a hotel and adding a gaming complex would be a shot in the financial arm for Ohio and others thought the opposite, especially those that had political ties to the Ohio lottery. The right posture was needed. A decent push was needed to educate the public.

Palmino Franco, a proud Marine veteran, had the expertise and the vision to accomplish the feat, but it wouldn't be easy to convince voters to go along with his plan. Mr. Franco would name expediency, reality, and honesty as measures needed. For sure Ohio desperately needed to keep money in Ohio and have an attraction that would lure tourists to the Buckeye State.

Doing his own fact finding without a troop of staff; he kept a low profile. Franco's goal was to select the most favorable territory. Lakefront acreage would be best. Lake Erie offered many favorable qualities. It had many large population centers on the south shore. It was clean and offered decent summer recreation to boaters and fishermen. A casino bordering on the Great Lakes would profit from merchant marine and transient boaters traffic. Boaters from Canada could easily make a trip across the lake. As factories closed land was for sale in areas that would help to make the casino a magnet to attract supporting infrastructure.

Since property was for sale almost everywhere, Franco could buy prime territory at bargain prices. He thought just buying land next to Lake Erie; the property would soar in value. If it was near the casino, it had residual value.

His first move was to secure land in several communities. He scoured the areas along Lake Erie. Spending some time in Cuyahoga, Geauga, and Ashtabula counties, he could see they didn't compare to Lake County. Loraine, Erie, Sandusky, and Ottawa counties were viable targets. Of all the choice land, something had to separate one from the others. Maybe he was biased or just business smart; he wanted his casino to be located in Lake County, Ohio.

On a morning jog he ran about a mile passing Lake Erie College, a couple banks, and sprinted across the Painesville Park. His aide, Simone Porter, was back at Rider's Inn waiting for his return. She was his close friend and personal secretary as well as a business attorney.

While the park was nearly the same; the town's business structure had changed. The goofy one-way streets were gone. Family department stores had vanished, replaced by institutional buildings. To the left he saw the old court house. The post office was gone and converted into a judiciary building. His eye caught sight of the Lake County Commissioner's administration building. With an air of bravado, he thought he might as well see if any political personalities were inside the building.

The land he was interested in was situated in seven areas. Conneaut, Painesville, Painesville Township, Mentor, the City of Lakewood, Chardon, and Lorain all had property at fire sale prices. He wrote most of Cleveland off because of their politics problems, although it was still a major Ohio city and certainly couldn't be completely expunged.

He had big casino plans, but wasn't ready to lay out the cards, until he was sure that voters would accept his concept. He needed someone with political experience to worm their way into the Ohio political apparatus.

Lake County was more interesting than the other areas just for the fact that he grew up in Painesville. Harvey High School, being his alma mater, carried a badge of honor. He played some of the most spirited football games against Riverside, Madison, and Fairport.

If Lake County was part of the big picture and his plan was to succeed, he needed leaders with a vision of the future on his side. Surely the county commissioners fit this mold.

He took the elevator to the commissioner's floor and walked in on the staff without an invitation. Franco was never afraid to open a door that said 'EMPLOYEES ONLY.'

Franco's casual introduction didn't weigh mighty on the staff, but his entrance startled the staff. Perspiring and slightly out of breath, the usually flamboyant and outgoing Franco was dressed in sneakers and a jogging suit.

Brenda Clark happened to have her office door open. She looked up to see the handsome, middle-aged man standing among the staff.

Franco opened up with a pointed message. "Just stopped to say, hello, girls. I'm visiting and buying land in the area. I'm from Oregon. I'm doing some land speculating in Lake County. It seems like the whole country is suffering an economic meltdown. Property values are sliding; looks like Northern Ohio is facing the same selling pressure as the rest of the nation."

"Sir, you're in an employee area," said Mrs. Wheeler.

Unflinching, Franco continued.

"I try to buy foreclosures and property when the price is right. I'm interested in discussing some business with the commissioners. Are there any big shots around here?"

Philomena Wheeler, the veteran secretary of the office, casts her eyes on the open door and points towards Brenda Clark's office. A sign, Brenda Clark, was clearly visible.

"You'll have to make an appointment to see the commissioners, but Mrs. Clark might be willing to see you."

Mrs. Wheeler, sensing the bravado of the newcomer, knew Brenda would appreciate the opportunity to talk with a handsome middle aged man. Pairing up Brenda Clark with Mr. Franco would be in line since she knew Mrs. Clark's traits.

Franco wasted no time interpreting Mrs. Wheeler's signal. He spun around to face her office as Philomena called out to Mrs. Clark.

"Brenda, a man has some business to discuss."

Abruptly, Franco marches in the direction of Mrs. Clark's office. As he approaches the door, he looks straight at her.

Above her name the title next to the door indicated she was the department head.

"Hello there, Mrs. Clark, my name's Palmino Franco. Would you arrange a moment of the commissioner's time for a brief business discussion? If that's not possible, I'll have my attorney, Simone Porter, call and make an appointment," said the tycoon.

Brenda's response was short and to the point.

"The commissioners have a busy schedule today, Mr. Franco. Unfortunately, you'll have to get in line, but I would be glad to assist you if you have some questions."

Brenda was careful at first, but changed as his smile seemed to kiss her on the lips. Her business character changed. Joyful, perhaps ready to meltdown from his gaze, she was eagerly willing to offer her assistance. She reached out to him as he pulled out a business card.

"Well, here's my calling card. I'm from Oregon. I'm looking to invest in a new business. I haven't been back to Painesville in… well, in long time. I'm considering a new project for the area."

Brenda's eyes lit up. After she grabbed his card, she carefully read the details. Her eyes bugged out when she read casino developer.

Brenda asks, "Do you ready build casinos?"

Franco answers, "I know the people of Ohio don't like casinos, but you never know how economic times can change an attitude. I'll be requesting help. Maybe, Lake County would benefit if plans can be worked out."

Looking up again, she seized the moment. Although his jogging suit didn't portray wealth, she knew it wasn't Joe six pack standing in front of her. His watch and ring didn't come out of a Cracker Jack box. By his tone she could tell he was serious. Thinking to herself for a moment she calculates that this man was more than a standard businessman. The business card bore some proof. Trying to recapture the opening introduction, she backtracked. Her mind was working fast. She didn't want to lump him in with routine business types.

"Were you here long? Sometimes I get caught up; I'm so sorry. We're here for you, Mr. Franco. If you have anything that will benefit the county; we're here for you. My door is open as you can see."

Mr. Franco says, "I came here through the park and saw the administration sign. I'm just jogging through Painesville, but you're busy. Not to worry, I'll make future arrangements. You'll hear from me down the road."

Brenda makes an attempt to keep him in the office.

"The commissioners aren't here right now. Would you like to leave some information that I can give to them?"

At first his words seem to pierce the business balloon and calls out for something more. Perhaps going overboard she extends her hand almost dumping a wave of good tiding to the entrepreneur. The bachelor takes her hand as if signaling his delight. The two exchange friendly glances. A chemistry of the mind flashes for Brenda. Although the initial greeting was slightly corrosive, her mood changed to hearts. Graciously, he holds her hand for a moment.

Franco says, "Let me know when the commissioners have time to weigh in on a project. I'll be back."

With that Franco turned away and flipped a business card on the counter. The ladies watched, almost in a trance as he walked away.

Brenda was ready to melt. Half mesmerized, sizing him up to be over six feet tall. She grabbed her pencil, guessing his age to be about fifty. He was a forward thinker, definitely a mover and a shaker. No wait in this type of guy, she thought. As her thoughts ran wild, she visualizes their next meeting. He was muscular and attractive. Shaking her head, it took her more than a moment to cool down.

Mrs. Clark had a million and one tasks going on. Franco's visit caused her to retreat from the jobs at hand. Her paralegal training wouldn't let her miss any details, although in this case she really focused on the chance greeting. She made a notation of the visit and stuck the business card under her desk mat. Realizing the importance of who she was dealing with, she put a sticky note on the wall of her office. The note was short, **Franco's attorney, Simone Porter, will call later. Palmino Franco owns Oregon casino.**

Franco's trusted girlfriend and attorney, Simone Porter, had reserved two suites at Rider's Inn for the week. She thought Franco would only stay for a few days, but he mentioned the fact that he might say hello to a few old friends which could extend his stay. She understood.

Miss Porter always thought Mr. Franco would marry her. She worked a blackjack table at his casino when they met. They struck up a casual relationship and started dating. He paid her way through law school and she stayed with him. He paid her very well as his legal aid, but it was more than that. She was in love with him and he took care of her. She didn't need to battle in the courtroom.

The cozy inn dating back to the early 1800's was run by a successful business woman. When Miss Porter asked about Lake County, Judge Elaine Crane had plenty to say. The middle-aged owner of the inn spoke about the heritage of Lake County.

"Counselor, you're in the Western Reserve, an area of Ohio once owned by the State of Connecticut," says the judge. Her captivating speech amplified the significance of Rider's Inn.

Obvious to the attorney as she looked around was the elegance of the interior of the tavern. The rustic ornaments and well kept woodwork which predated the civil war was interesting and historic.

Mrs. Crane pointed out how the pioneers used the tavern as a stopping point.

"This tavern was part of an old stagecoach route. It's where beleaguered travelers could recover from the bumpy ride. I'm taking you back a long time ago. You could say Rider's Inn is an icon in Lake County. Rider's Inn is filled with stories of the past. Many dignitaries have stayed here. Any one of our eleven suites will help you regain your freshness. When you stay at Rider's Inn; you'll be part of a distinguished heritage." says the proud owner.

Simone listened as the judge added details of the Western Reserve.

"Painesville is the county seat. The Erie Indians roamed in Lake County before Ohio was a state. Brigadier General Moses Cleveland and Surveyor Seth Pease worked to tame this land. This inn has much to offer its guests."

Simone carefully listened to Judge Crane. Her hearty words raised the bar on a county that was ahead of the pack. She described Painesville and Mentor as two cities moving on up. The economic developers weren't sleeping at the wheel. Plans for a recreational park next to Lake Erie were beyond the drawing board stage.

After considerable dialogue Judge Crane closed by giving a tip to the young attorney. The tip was a coincidence that would play out in the plans for the future casino. She mentioned the strong personality of the county commissioners' paralegal secretary, Mrs. Brenda Clark.

"Make an appointment with Mrs. Clark. She's a bullhorn to the county commissioners. Her political reach likely extends to Columbus. Anyone looking to invest in Lake County will surly do well by her. She's that kind of woman. You want her on your team. She's a doer."

That evening, while eating dinner at Rider's Inn, Simone and Palmino conversed about the day's events. The topics varied. Mr. Franco had plenty to say. He talked about Ohio's ancestors.

He says, "Many people from Connecticut and New Hampshire were captured by the Indians. My great, great, great grandmother was forced to marry into Indian tribes. I think I have Indian blood in my veins. Could be I'm part Delaware Indian."

Simone caught on to his words. She added her thoughts to displace the notion that he somehow had Indian blood in his veins.

"I know what you're aiming to do, boss. You better save the Indian story. I have some good news. Your dream about establishing a casino in Ohio got a little rosier. There's a woman at the Lake County commissioner's office that might help you. Her name is Brenda Clark."

Palmino's ears tuned in as he rubbed his chin almost disbelieving her comment.

Simone continued, "Mrs. Crane said this woman has good connections with Ohio politicians. I think she's the Indian you need in your camp."

He didn't tell Simone that he just met the woman. He held his thought for a moment. Then, after hearing her story, Mr. Franco decided the heavenly stars might be aligning.

"You say her name is Brenda Clark. Simone, you're not going to believe this. I met this woman this morning. I stopped at the county commissioners' office while on my jog. I liked who I saw today, but don't jump the gun. I can see Lake County has hired good people. We'll use Brenda Clark. You make the arrangements. We'll meet with Mrs. Clark and the commissioners. Write this down, Simone. Lake County is going to get a casino. We'll get Mrs. Clark on our team. We might not lure her away from Lake County, but we'll use her influence to reach Columbus," says Franco.

In a diary Simone entered the dialogue of the day, including time. Franco was a stickler for keeping track of people that surround his plan.

Each day Simone and Palmino constructed bits and pieces of the operation.

Franco had a list of the properties that could be bought. A map listed the locations.

After studying a map, he was sure about his decision. He puts his finger on the exact location of the first casino.

"Right there next to the lake, Simone, Lake County is the perfect mate for a hotel and casino. Look, they're fixing the roads, building a new hospital, a sports park, and this is a perfect point. It's a place where tourists and boat travelers can stop. Lake Erie adds beauty, summer recreation, and sports tournaments. You're going to see the bigger picture in a moment.

"Look at my map. Let's not stop. Simone, I see several areas to locate other recreational parks. These will all work together in Ohio and the nice thing about the whole concept. It's for summer sports and winter sports. We're building a sporting empire not just another place to gamble. It'll all be situated between Las Vegas and Atlantic City. They'll want to join with us."

Miss Porter could see the shine in the hotel magnet's eyes. She loved when he acted this way.

Palmino says, "You and I will meet with Brenda Clark; we're building an empire."

Simone knew it. Her guy was on to something big. She tried to hold the excitement inside. Franco told her to act like an attorney, a personal secretary, and expert business advisor. He didn't want her looking like a wife or girlfriend. That was a tall order for the blond haired beauty.

A ridged decision maker, Franco had a bona fide plan to locate a hotel and casino on the shore of Lake Erie. Although others tried to accomplish the same without success, he wasn't discouraged. His mind was made up. The time was right. The high rise hotel was right for Lake County in spite of the economy.

Although the Ohio casino portion of his idea would be a tough project, the plan had promise. Franco had a savvy diplomat to maneuver inside the halls of Columbus.

"Money, Simone, is what the politicians in Columbus need. We have money. Brenda Clark is going to lay out my case for a casino, even multiple casinos in Ohio. Now is the time. I know how we can operate in Ohio, Pennsylvania, and New York."

Palmino Franco and Simone Porter discussed the plan for three more hours.

The next day Brenda Clark's phone rang. On the other end was Attorney Simone Porter. She wanted to meet as soon as possible.

Mrs. Clark quickly glanced at her notes and realized that the lawyer was Mr. Franco's legal advisor. Wasting no time, Mrs. Clark agreed to meet at Rider's Inn. They had much information to discuss.

They met that afternoon for lunch. Because Mr. Franco was inspecting property near Lake Erie, he wasn't with the ladies right away.

The meeting was semi-cordial for an initial business meeting. It didn't go off as well as expected. Mrs. Clark was a little flippant even covetous because Miss Porter was younger, beautiful, and perhaps well suited in her relationship with Mr. Franco.

Sensing that Mrs. Clark might have an eye on Mr. Franco, Simone tossed out some personal information against the wishes of Mr. Franco. Miss Porter made the fact known that Mr. Franco paid for her education and she shared a close friendship with him.

This only convinced Brenda to try out her bag of tricks if Mr. Franco comes to the meeting. Although they didn't hit it off very well the jockeying turned a corner when Mr. Franco walked in on the ladies. He detected a strained mood. He livened up the spirit by ordering a bottle of Chardonnay. Next, he talked about purchasing land in two Lake County townships. This set the stage for building a hotel and casino.

They conversed for the next two hours. Mr. Franco requested that Mrs. Clark build a casino support group. He would hire her to act as a liaison.

She wouldn't leave the commissioners, but agreed to be a link between Columbus and Lake County. With that role filled, Franco asked her to meet with a Columbus attorney on Saturday to study gambling rules and laws of Ohio. She agreed to go to Columbus and meet Attorney Dom DeLargo, who was a low level government official.

Finally, he asked Mrs. Clark to join the pro-casino committee and attend a few casino rallies that he was forming. Again she readily agreed.

Simone wasn't so happy with the invitations and Franco could tell by her attitude that his advisor was slightly upset.

Finally, the meeting broke up. As they were about to leave, Brenda Clark told Franco that she has a boyfriend, Richard Stern, who would be happy to help with the casino plan. This was a coincidence that Franco was delighted to hear, although he didn't foresee the trouble it would bring.

Chapter 6
Palmino Franco's Idea

Palmino Franco's wholesome personality and business sense were qualities that helped him build an empire in Oregon. Although luck was a factor he knew how to trade and hire talent. Other reasons for his success were found in the Franco heritage. His family roots dated back beyond the early seventeenth century. His great, great, great, grandfather inherited coins and Indian artifacts. He passed down many collector pieces to preserve the family numismatic collection. Family moved west from Connecticut. His great grandfather settled in Painesville. Franco learned the art of bartering through his grandfather.

Mr. Franco graduated from Harvey High School. He was picked to be a Marine as a drafted soldier during the Viet Nam War. Surviving the war was one accomplishment. After serving his country he moved around a bit. Getting serious about his future, he graduated from Toledo University and was playing baseball for a short time before moving out West. His successes multiplied in Oregon.

Politically the nation was contracting to one party rule. Franco saw opportunity in high unemployment and home foreclosures. He could afford to expand because his Oregon hotel and casino was running in the black and could function without him while he investigates the next horizon.

His experienced subordinates would run the Lewis and Clark Hotel and Casino while he assembles the eastern team. With an eye on Ohio, now it was time to turn his attention to an eastern front.

All casinos had something in common. People will either like them or vote against them. As with the citizens in Oregon he thought it would only be a matter of time before Ohioans would get over the negative stigma of a casino. His operation would be for families, sportsmen, and people of all ages.

His general approach was a simple idea. He would build a hotel for the huge summertime influx of tournament athletes. Baseball, softball, soccer, volleyball, and basketball teams would converge in Northeastern Ohio throughout the seasons. The casino would be built at the same time with the expectation that tourists would populate the hotel and tournament spectators would help feed the casino if people voted in favor of a casino.

Weather was a troubling factor. When the season changed to winter, the casino would need to hold its own. For this reason a multitude of winter activities would be needed and available to the public. Sled riding, cross-country skiing, and fishing indoors were just a few ideas. Social activities, plays and concerts at the hotel amphitheater, would feature a wide range of talent from state colleges. He wanted America's families to engage in physical workouts. To this end he had outdoor exercise areas in the summer and indoor games during the winter. An Olympic pool and a horticulture museum provided activities during inclement weather.

The hotel's theme was focused on the idea of staying physically fit even though the main restaurant was not afraid to offer some extravagant meals.

A winter fort, a senior center, could house a multitude of activities. Equipment to exercise the mind and body would keep elderly vacationers from turning to the warm weather in Florida. An arrangement was made with the support of county transportation to shuttle folks in and out for special senior occasions. If he could keep large groups of senior citizens in his place for one, two, or three weeks at a time at bargain prices, they would help support the casino.

Because Palmino Franco grew up in Painesville, Ohio, it was natural for him to stay a fierce competitor in sports. This characteristic appealed to many men and women growing up during the fifties, sixties, and beyond. It was handed down from parents and grandparents.

Ohio was well endowed with money derived from World War II. The bread basket state in Middle America helped feed the nation and was an industrial titan. During the era people could see Lake County, Ohio was growing faster than other counties in Ohio.

Franco knew that sports in Ohio had a special meaning. Two of the fun spots as he grew up during the fifties and sixties were in Cleveland. Professional football and baseball were still games that most could afford. Pro football wasn't sullied by drugs and neither was baseball. Both sports were inexpensive to go and see, especially major league baseball. The Municipal Stadium in Cleveland provided a home for some decent, sometimes raucous entertainment. The ballpark and pro ballplayers sharpened Franco's aspiration to be a baseball player. Unfortunately, Franco's pitching arm couldn't hold up. He only advanced to Class AA, but he retained the competitive edge.

Franco didn't maintain contact with many Ohioans. When Richard Stern vacationed in Oregon he met Franco and gave an overview of Lake County.

After doing extensive research Mr. Franco called Stern and discussed Ohio sports. Some of the conversation focused on Lake County and the surrounding area.

Stern said that over the years, when Franco was away, Lake County high schools nurtured many quality athletes as well as academic achievers. Although that wasn't so unusual, city, towns, and villages were responding to the sports movement.

Because child obesity was on the rise, schools increased their emphasis on sports programs for all ages. This flashed over to local governments, who also chipped in. He added that more and more private weight training facilities were adding exercise equipment. A trend was growing.

Stern couldn't name them all. He mentioned Lake County's hot spots for sports as being in Mentor, Willoughby, Painesville, Perry, and Madison. These were five places addressing the challenge to keep Lake County's youths physically fit. Stern said it wasn't just the young nor was it just confined to Lake County. Chardon High School was ahead of their time. That school was one of the first to build a beautiful stadium. Another nice stadium for track, football, and soccer was at Ashtabula Lakeside. Ashtabula County was making news by adding a huge sports facility.

Stern said, "Mr. Franco, I write about sports and photograph sporting events. Team sports will likely expand if the economy gets better."

Franco had a practical idea to adjust to the economic conditions. His operation would flex to expand or contract as needed to meet the size and type of game player. Events would change. One week might feature boating and fishing. Another week baseball and softball tournaments would be the main event. Soccer, basketball, and volleyball tournaments could be going on at the same time.

If the weather was bad, the casino, restaurants, and shows would entertain the crowd. Low cost shuttles to shopping centers and museums would be available.

The new style of casino playing would be a blend of nature and sports. Gambling would be secondary. Shows and art would receive the greatest amount of advertising. Sports players and spectators could relax in the hotel and casino after the games.

Mr. Franco talked about the sports research his staff conducted. They found that sports teams were forming all over. Columbus was a growing area. Cleveland was shrinking. This was affecting his future plans. Young and middle aged people were converting to team sports.

Whether people were bicycling, running distance races, or competing in traditional team sports the numbers were increasing. If the base of spectators and participants could be attracted to one location, Franco's concept would be successful.

Richard said, "Kids in Lake County are definitely playing more team sports. If there's a down size in middle and high school sports, its pay to play. I get requests to take pictures. I can see the parents are getting involved."

Franco still had some fun watching major league sports. While it still attracted his interest, the lower level games were more important to him. This was a common point in their discussion. It was clear they both understood what was happening.

As Franco continued to study Ohio sports in general, he could see sports parks were springing up randomly. Football was still a fall giant, but in the spring and summer youth soccer, baseball, and softball were prince, king, and queen. In the winter, especially in Northeast Ohio, basketball, volleyball, and indoor soccer were very important.

Something else cemented his reasons for building in Ohio. He liked the parent's attitude toward helping keep kids of all ages physically fit. He could understand reasons for parents, teachers, and coaches placing a high value on physical activity in addition to academics. Americans were getting fat.

Tournament play for youths would allow boys and girls to stay ahead of the physical fitness curve.

Franco had a summary in front of him. People are supporting baseball and softball teams. People of all ages are coming to play summertime tournaments in Lake County. To complement this growing base of sports' enthusiasts a new wave of sport facilities had arrived. Franco wanted to be part of the picture, but he could add another chip to the pot, an Ohio casino. Richard Stern knew it. A casino located near a modern sports park with multiple fields could be the future that sparks a new wave of growth in Northeast Ohio.

After the conversation, Franco had one other thought lodged in his mind that he didn't bring up. A painful journey was about to begin. The hotel and casino idea would work well with a sports complex, but adversaries would be out there. Franco knew they would try to stop him.

Chapter 7
Agents, Mob, and Politics

Supervisor Cliff Moses knew the day was coming when the air between Micovich and Wright would become stale. He knew the characteristics of his agents.

Wright was a ladies man. It was only a matter of time before he got in hot water. One way or another that was his nature. Reckless at times, a playboy during the off hours, Wright often found trouble as his partner, Ron Roman, would attest. Moses used the two agents when there was a hint of danger. Roman kept Wright in check as much as possible. Roman was no Saint Christopher. The two men were a perfect match, Roman's brawn and brains coupled with Wright's savvy and bravery. Roman, a portly agent, was no man to mess with. Wright, a lightning fast sharpshooter, won numerous awards while competing in handgun contests.

Moses could confidently trust the men to follow orders even though they would put a scalpel to some of the department rules. 'We'll be there, when times are tough' was their motto, but fully expect them to be fishing somewhere along the way.

When Paula called with word about Monica and the baby, Moses was all ears. Paula was beyond excited. Although Moses was excited, he needed to calm Paula down. During her talkative burst she unloaded the verdict between Monica and Bill.

The dashed love affair, it was no surprise to him. In fact this was good news. Cliff didn't like the personal mingling between Monica and Bill. The end to the romantic tango would be beneficial to the department. This would mean the team of Wright and Roman would be whole and not distracted by a third wheel. He held his tongue with the expectation that the love affair would whither on the vine. He was right as usual.

Cliff had been reviewing the files of Monica's cases. He wanted to make sure everything was in order before he left the country. She uncovered some phony record keeping and then traced the operation to some politicians. The political graft ran deep.

Monica Micovich upset the apple cart by uncovering bid rigging. The corruption involved mayors and a governor's advisor. The ring of politicians started turning on each other as she exposed the plot. Even an illegal numbers game was uncovered.

The busts infuriated the godfather. The mafia was losing ground. He needed the politicians in order to win construction bids.

A meeting between the godfather of the syndicate and his lieutenants was heated. Seeing the godfather's face was a signal that all was not well. The red faced leader of the MidAmerican syndicate was angry. Obviously perturbed, veins popping out on his forehead, he prompts his assistant to speak about the trouble.

Andy Walsh asks, "Do you remember, John Paul Beach, boss? They call him, Beaner. He shuttles between Chicago and Cleveland to straighten out our bookies if they get sticky fingers. He says that a good looking broad, an FBI agent, Monica Micovich, is causing all the fuss. Beaner says you can identify her because she's pregnant. She works at the Cleveland Justice Center every now and then."

The godfather speaks, "This isn't good. Our reputation is at stake. The politicians want protection. What the hell is going on, boys? Are we afraid of a pregnant woman?"

The lieutenants weren't laughing as the godfather made his points. His book making operations and contract peddlers were forced to shutdown because of Agent Micovich's investigations. She had dug into the heart of the syndicate's operation. She took down a mayor. This made the politicians less cooperative and she helped put a few mobsters in jail. The crime family was getting nervous. This set the wheels in motion for a counter attack.

"A pregnant agent is doing all this, Walsh. We need to stop this problem." Walsh threw a picture of Monica on the table.

"Beaner gave me this picture, boss. This is the woman. He says that he'll find out where she lives."

The godfather holds up the picture to show his traveling lieutenants, Boris Gedeon and Lou Looma.

Gedeon and Looma had some tough luck in their past. The career con men would cheat their own mothers. The length of their misdeeds was long; crime was a way of life. They had already found shelter in their lives. It was behind prison walls. The short stint at the Conneaut Correctional Institution was a mild sedative. It wasn't long enough for the career minded villains.

Both men were portly, overeaters. Boris was tall, an ex-weightlifter, who joined the Russian mob in order to escape the Iron Curtain. Lou was fond of horse racing. He made friends with Boris at the track and joined the Chicago mob because of his banking background. He was good with numbers, but his sticky fingers landed him in prison for six months. He used the banks money to finance some gambling, but paid back all the money. The godfather used them together to investigate book making operations and apply pressure when needed.

"Boris, when we find out where she lives, she will pay a price for upsetting our operation. You visit the Cleveland area and see what's going on. We don't want the feds doing any more damage to the operation, so we need to be careful."

The godfather sat for a moment in silence before he spoke.

"Take Lou with you. We need to upset this woman's life a little without bring the fed down on us. Start with something small, Boris.

A house fire would be nice. A house warming event will do. Torch her house, but make it look like an accident. Let's cause her a little anxiety. This might slow her down."

Boris answers, "We'll head to Cleveland, boss. I'll handle this problem."

"Do that, Boris. See if you can warm things up. We will call you with her address. Make sure you call us back when you're finished."

Chapter 8
Michael and House Hunting Baby

On the third day, Monica and little Michael were released from the hospital. Monica holds the baby as Paula, babbling away, drives down Lake Shore Boulevard. They travel past East 305th and turn down Bayridge Boulevard heading to Monica's house.

Paula was clearly overjoyed with escorting mom and the baby home. She opened up with volunteerism. "I'll be the nanny for the next six months, Monica, and then I'll be the babysitter. Isn't he just a sweetheart?"

Finding a pause in Paula's talkative barrage Monica asks, "Will you be the Godmother?"

"Are you kidding me? This little guy is so special. Who's going to be the godfather? Oh, Cliff would be honored I'm sure."

"Wow, Paula, I forgot to ask Cliff. I'll call him later. I have to tell him about a reporter who was snapping pictures of me. I'm a little worried some perverted journalist will splash my picture with Michael on one of those internet sites or in a magazine. Wouldn't it be just my luck to see a headline, 'Agent busts the mob's book making operation' at a newsstand."

The conversation between Monica and Paula turned to the cases that Monica was working on prior to departing the department on maternity leave.

"No doubt about it, Paula. I did bust some of the syndicates favored methods of extorting money from the public. Maybe they'll put a contract out on me."

Disturbed, Paula answers, "Let's not go there, OK."

Baby Michael was wrapped in a blue Finnish shawl Paula purchased at a Fairport Harbor festival. She saved it for the baby. Grabbing her cell phone, she was so proud of the baby wrapped in the shawl, Paula snapped a picture. She felt that she was witnessing a great gift from God. Inspired by her faith, she said a silent prayer for Monica and Michael.

Once at home everything seemed in order. The nursery was decorated in blue. Paula spent the night with her friend. The next day Paula was back on the job.

Monica's lost love was replaced by a new life. What seemed like an impossible time to drop a substitute father was not that bad. Little Michael warmed her heart. He did the entertaining, providing plenty of special moments for mom. The realization, bringing a baby home, was almost a miracle. Although she suffered a letdown, Monica realized how lucky she was. The anticipation and labor was behind her. She had great expectations for Michael.

Taking advantage of the maturity leave, she had ample time to think about her next move in life. Ideas ran through her mind. One of Monica's key skills was making tough decisions. She decided to start Michael's life where the real father lives. Fairport Harbor was a quiet town not too far from work. Monica knew Mr. Stern was getting help from Father Pete to control his alcoholism. He joined AA. If he found himself, he could be a positive influence.

She didn't tell her partner because Paula worked so hard helping her set up the nursery.

Finding a buyer for her home wasn't a huge problem because the neighbor always wanted to buy her house. She offered him a deal he couldn't refuse.

Homes were for sale everywhere because of the banking industry's loaning practices. Many home owners bought houses at outrageously high prices and then the housing bubble burst. The economy was spiraling out of control. Monica quickly picked up a decent property with two houses on the land in Fairport Harbor. It had a large garage with a loft on top. She could live in the back house if the front house needed work.

She called Paula with the news of her purchase.

"Paula, I'm moving. I sold my house. I'm going east, moving to Fairport Harbor."

"What's that? Monica, did I hear you right? Fairport Harbor, is that what you said?"

Monica answers quickly, "I love the small town. I go to church there. I found a decent place right by the high school."

Paula, still not believing, asks again. "Are you sure about what you're going? You have a nice place in Willowick. We just got it ready for the baby."

Paula was quick to point out that Richard Stern lives there.

"What about Mr. Stern, Monica? Aren't you trying to keep him away from Michael?"

Monica quickly addressed that question? Her dashed experience with Bill Wright removed the question mark about fathers.

"Richard will find out he's the father one of these days. He's on the birth certificate. Michael needs a father. Fathers don't grow on trees. I thought I'd found Mr. Wonderful. Bill turned out to be a jerk. I won't say anything to Richard, but like I said, he'll find out eventually and he's the real dad. I just have to accept that. If he can straighten out, he might be a good father. I can't change what I did ten months ago."

Paula was concern about what was waiting down the road and she kept asking questions.

"What are you going to do when or if he wants visitation?"

"Ohio has child support laws and protection laws. He'll probably keep quiet if he knows I'm willing to pay all the child care bills. Do you think he made a fortune on reward money?"

Paula adds, "Are you after child support?"

"No, not really, I might as well keep the option open, Paula."

"Well, you asked if he's loaded. So my answer is, he's probably loaded, but not with money. He got reward money from the bureau, we know that much. Maybe you should get some of the reward money or sue him for a wrongful sperm injection."

"That's cute, Paula. You're a real comforting soul. I have to go, bye."

Paula doesn't quit. She continues, "Monica, he has to pay."

"Listen, Paula, I don't want him coming over. So let's keep this a secret, ok."

"My lips are sealed, partner," says Paula, although she knows Monica isn't telling all.

Paula agrees to Monica's wish, but fate was to intervene.

Monica didn't waste any time moving out. She found the house she wanted and laid down a sizable installment. She contracted movers and sold many items to the new owner. After two days of clearing out small items she handed the house keys to her neighbor, Doug Patterson, and moved to Fairport Harbor. With Paula helping the transition was swift.

Chapter 9
Seeking Revenge

Boris camped out near the Justice Center in Cleveland. Fishing for information, he asked a hot dog vendor if he knew any of the people in the two photographs he had. He examined the second photo closely.

"Oh, yah! Monica Micovich, that's her alright. Wow, she's knocked up. Wish I was her husband. I think maybe she's a big shot lawyer."

Boris was surprised by his answer.

"She's a lawyer! Is that right?"

The vendor adds, "And a nice dresser; classy woman, foxy, you know what I mean. She was here a few months ago. I thought she put on some weight, but I wasn't about to say anything. You know how women are. Yah, yah, that's her, Monica, I wanna be twenty-five again and find a hot chick like that. She comes out and grabs a sandwich once in a while, but I haven't seen her in a couple months."

Boris puffs on a cigar and answers, 'Thanks pal, give me a couple dogs."

The mobster called back to his boss with the news.

"She definitely works at the Justice Center, boss. The hotdog vendor fingered her when I showed him the picture."

"Good news, Boris, we just got her address. She lives in Willowick. Write this down. She lives off East 305th Street."

The godfather calls out the address and points out one other fact.

"There's a park near her home. They call it Dudley Park. I have an idea."

The godfather saw a convenient way to send Agent Monica a payback message.

The godfather asks. "Do you remember those remote planes we were flying at my villa?"

"Yah, boss, I remember. We used a GPS controller to torch Fisheye's car," says Boris.

"That's right, Boris. The planes are even better now. Now they'll really explode when they crash. We added a better igniter on the nose and a carriage on each wing. It'll carry twice as much fuel."

"Drive back here. I want you to practice flying the planes a few times. You're going to be a kamikaze pilot. You're too much of a fat ass to fly, Boris, but flying a plane by remote control you don't have to be in the cockpit. You're going to have an accident in Willowick, Ohio. Do you know what's going to happen, Boris?

He answers, "I'm going to fly that baby into her house."

The godfather says, "Good; that'll be the first warning that bitch gets, maybe her last. No screw ups on this one. Tell me you got it?"

"I got it, boss."

"Good, come back to the villa, Boris."

Once back at the godfather's villa, Boris practiced flying each remote controlled plane. First, he sent it under a clothesline and then into the barn and out the back. His confidence was increasing with each flyby. After three days of flying, it was time to show the boss. His rented Cadillac was parked in the field with the back doors open. Boris wanted the godfather to witness his expertise at flying.

Boris asked the godfather to watch a circus act he had planned. The boss and the lieutenants gathered outside to watch Boris perform. The remote controlled plane made several dummy passes over the Cadillac.

The wind was gusting slightly which moved the plane off course on the last attempt. It passes over and above the trunk of the car.

"Don't worry, boss, the wind is shifting. I'm going to reposition the caddy," said Boris.

He moved the car so that the breeze would flow through the open doors. The mobsters were anticipating the worst.

The godfather said, "I'm laying a thousand bucks the fat ass burns his car." The boys wouldn't take the bet, but they were amused.

Boasting, Boris explains, "Gentlemen, I'm about to make aviation history. This is a stunt only a highly trained remote control expert such as me should try. Now I know what it's like to be a CIA operator in Afghanistan."

The godfather could see the cockiness and foolhardiness overtaking Boris' act.

"The imbecile will screw this up, boys. You watch," said the godfather.

The godfather and his lieutenants stood at attention anticipating disaster. Boris had the plane in the air for another flyby. This time the plane was on target, flying dead over the top of the Cadillac's rear doors. As the plane circled for the grand finale, it ran out of gas. Boris was forced to glide the plane in for an emergency landing.

"Damn, it's out of fuel, boss."

"Boris," called the godfather, "How many planes do you have?"

"Two, boss, no worry, I'll just refuel," said Boris.

The godfather had seen enough. He gave the final instruction.

"Boris, you have two planes and no brains. When you get back to Ohio, make sure the plane you're going to use has fuel. You got it."

"OK, boss, I got it. I'm leaving tonight."

Chapter 10
Babysitters and a House Fire

Moving from Willowick to Fairport Harbor was a transition to less busy streets, a slower town rather than an upbeat suburb. Monica's new neighborhood was filled with adorable old houses mostly built in the early 1900's.

Her main house sat ten yards off a sidewalk lined street. The main dwelling was a white colonial with a large front porch. The small house in the back sat next to a converted barn. The barn turned garage had a loft on top.

Getting used to the old house took time. The neighborhood was mostly quiet until the children came outside. Fond memories returned of visiting the grandparent's modest home when they were alive. Her grandpa's house was similarly built.

A speedy purchase of the homes was needed when she bought the property. The property was selling at a foreclosure price. Because of this, she didn't go over the buildings with an eye for minor structural problems.

The old house had a few deficiencies. After a few days of living in the house, she was alerted to some pesky annoyances.

Some floorboards squeaked. A slight dip was noted near the kitchen sink. A similar noise was true of floorboards going up the stairs to the bedrooms. In Michael's room a window didn't slide very well.

Skipper

Door locks were going to be changed as a first order of business, but she would have to wait a few days for the locksmith. A secondary lock would have to do in the meantime.

Creaky steps and floor boards signaled loose wood. She would ascend and descend the steps to the second floor with care for fear she would wake the baby. She memorized the pattern of squeaks in the house and walked as if in a minefield. She started listing the problems to solve. On the list were things she thought she could do.

Monica set out working on the problems. If she was going to replace the carpet, the annoying noise had to be fixed. Thinking she could quiet the floor noise herself, she gathered tools for the work. After a couple hours of toiling with hammer and nails, frustration was mounting. The baby was awake from the pounding.

Rocking Michael in her arms put him back to sleep. She could understand a baby and noisy home repairs wouldn't mix very well.

She retreated to the porch steps with Michael to regain her composer. Jotting down a list of problems helped her decide that she needed carpenters to handle the repairs. Since she saved a bundle of money on the purchase price and made a tidy some off her previous home; she could afford to farm out the work.

The neighbors living near Monica heard the pounding and saw her sitting on the front steps. Some folks were nosy and others were anxious to meet the new resident. One and then two, they nonchalantly drifted over. First, a friendly neighbor next door came over.

Mrs. Luoma greeted Monica.

"Hello, I'm Jeannie Luoma, your neighbor. I teach at the Fairport High School."

Monica was glad to meet the neighbor and potential friend. After cordial introduction, she called attention to her home repair troubles.

"Hi, Jeannie, I'm Monica Micovich. My baby boy and I just moved in. His name is Michael. I'm hoping or should I say I'm desperately in need of a good carpenter. I'm sure you heard my hammering. I've been pounding away on loose boards. I give up. Do you know of any local outfits that can handle home repairs?"

Mrs. Luoma quickly mentioned Harbor Construction.

They talked for several minutes. Then a couple of Mrs. Luoma's former students came over.

Mrs. Luoma said, "Girls, meet your new neighbor, Monica Micovich. She has a baby boy, Michael."

Rachel Jeavons and Taylor Landies introduced themselves. The group observed Michael, who was dosing and oblivious to all the attention he was getting. The girls offered to baby-sit in the future. Monica was glad to hear that offer. A babysitter was definitely needed.

Soon two more neighbors came over to meet the new Fairporters.

Questions and answers kept coming up about home repairs. The neighbors agreed and the consensus of advice was that Monica should call Harbor Construction, so her choice was made easy. She would call them.

After talking with the neighbors, she discovered that the girls worked part time at the coffee shop at Great Lakes Mall. She didn't want to always bother Paula. Having the girls as neighbors would make finding a babysitter much easier.

Monica called the Harbor Construction Company. She explained the problems to Steve Babb who offered to personally estimate the job. After the initial discussion, Monica had a decision to make. Time would be a factor.

The front house was going to need a certain amount of immediate repairs which would take some time. Then there was painting that she wanted to do. With all the proposed work to be done noise, dust, and smelly paint fumes would be expected, so she temporarily moved into the guest house so the baby and she wouldn't be bothered as much. She figured if she'd be in the guest house for a couple weeks or a month; it was well worth it.

Harbor Construction's boss, Steve Babb, pointed out other concerns, sticky doors and loose tile in the bathroom. Since he was so knowledgeable, a green light was given. She was determined to correct the problems one after another. "Let's get the floors fixed first and then move on to other fixes," Mr. Babb.

Mr. Babb added, "My partner, Terry Vale, runs the roofing business. Harbor Roofing is his operation. Just give us a call anytime you have any of these problems. Terry lives in town and I graduated from Fairport Harding. We know all about Fairport Harbor houses. In fact my dad was a math teacher and superintendent of the schools in Fairport. He coached football, too."

She adds to the conversation. "I grew up in Mentor. Went to high school at Lake Catholic and graduated from St. Leo College in Florida. You probably never heard of St. Leo, but it's a Roman Catholic college."

Mr. Babb says, "Mr. Vale lived in Florida years ago. I'm sure Terry knows about St. Leo. You hired the right team, Mrs. Micovich. We'll get the job done."

"Well, that's wonderful, Steve. Oh, by the way I'm not married. It's Monica Micovich, Miss Micovich."

Monica and baby Michael settled in the rear home. It seemed like some things were returning to normal. The stress of moving to Fairport Harbor was almost behind her. However, an uneasiness was about to return.

One Week Later

A seismic vibration came to light when she read the local newspaper. A particular caption caught her eye. With eyes zooming in on the headline after scrutinizing Willowick's name, greater attention was given the article. The street where Monica used to live was in the story. She knew many residents who lived near her. After reading the article she was as curious as a cat. She picked up the phone and called her sidekick, Paula.

Monica asks. "Hey, Paula, do you want to go for a ride with Michael and me? I just read an article in the paper about a house fire in Willowick on my old street."

Paula could tell from Monica's voice that they weren't going to

Willowick just to look at a house fire. It was something more. Even though Monica's a mother, she's still a crime fighter and Paula knew that was the driving force. Cleverly, Paula baits her partner's prowess, which was agitated anyhow.

Paula asks, "Are you burning up with curiosity, partner?"

Monica replies in a matter of fact. "Well, you take a look, if you have the newspaper handy. Look at the headlines on the bottom of page one and keep reading.

House Fire in Willowick
House fire is caused by model plane.
Guts a two story house on Bayridge.

"Wow, Monica! A model plane flies into a house and destroys it. Was it someone you knew?

"Yes! My neighbor," yelps Monica, "Doug Patterson's name is mentioned, but it didn't say which house. Let's go check it out."

The two agents loaded Michael into the van. They gabbed for the twenty minute ride. As they turned on Bayridge Street anticipation ended the conversation. Shock greeted them as they drove to the seen of the fire.

"My God, it's my old house!

"Monica, this is weird."

"I can't believe this has happened to my old neighbor. Poor Doug Patterson, let's stop and talk with him."

As the van pulls onto Mr. Patterson's driveway, he opens the front door and walks to the van. His facial expression tells a story of a brooding man. The reception is slightly cool, which alerts Monica that Doug is very distraught over his misfortune. Monica tried to find the words to express her shock. Thinking for a few seconds, she hops out of the van and offers a few comforting words.

The hug is greeted by disdain.

"Monica, did you come to see my misfortune? Doug asked.

"Doug, I'm so sorry. My friend, Paula and I saw the article in the newspaper. I wanted to find out for myself how this all happened. I brought Michael along for the ride. It's not a joy ride that's for sure. "

Monica points to Paula, who waves her hand.

Paula chips in with consoling words. "Hello, Mr. Patterson. This isn't a nice way to meet, but we want to look and see if we can be of any help."

Mr. Patterson politely waves, but his face reveals anguish.

Paula moves to the driver's side seat, carefully listening to the conversation.

He has much to say to Agent Micovich and makes some striking remarks. Mr. Patterson said that the fire is under investigation for arson.

Mr. Patterson declares, "This is a bad joke. I'm not laughing. Who would fly a model plane loaded with gas into the picture window of my house? Except, maybe they thought it was your house, Monica."

Monica didn't want to go in that direction. She turns her questions back to Patterson.

"Do you have any enemies, Mr. Patterson? Anybody threaten you lately?" Monica asks.

"No! Fire officials found a burned out hulk of a model airplane," explains Patterson.

He continues, "The plane was messed up pretty bad, but they think it had extra fuel tanks mounted on it. Something isn't right. Somebody wanted to cause a fire or did they want to keep the plane in the air longer? I suppose the plane could have malfunctioned, but why? I have my own theory."

"What's that?" Paula asks.

"Two boys talked with a man who had a model plane at Dudley Field, Chuck Ferline's boys. They're witnesses."

"Wow, we have witnesses," says Paula.

Doug got to the point in the conversation where he needed to vent.

"I think somebody is after you, Monica. This stranger thought this was your house and crashed the plane through your bay window. That's what I think, Monica."

"I won't rule anything out, Doug, but right now it's all coincidental," says Monica.

The agents were inquisitive. Doug's explanation couldn't be ruled out.

Mr. Patterson says, "You're not supposed to fly remote planes in a residential area. This guy had a purpose in mind. Tell me, Monica. Who's after you?"

Monica answers, "Doug, we investigate crime; many crimes in many locations are the nature of this business. I can't rule out anything."

Doug didn't stop. He had more to say.

"The boys up the street said that a man driving a large white car was testing his model plane's engine at Dudley Field. At least that's what the man said when the boys asked. Then this guy sends the plane airborne. The boys thought it unusual because the man drove off with the remote control and the plane was still in the air."

Monica looked at Paula. The astonished look was apparent. Wanting to believe that this could be retaliation or racially motivated, Monica asked a question.

"Mr. Patterson, I mean, Doug, I know you referee boxing, you officiate high school wrestling matches, and you're a black man. Do you think a hate crime is a possibility?"

"No, Monica. I think somebody hates you."

Monica asked once more, "Has anyone threatened you lately?"

Mr. Patterson went on the offensive and came right out after her. Doug didn't like the insinuation. He shot back.

"I'm fair, Monica! We were neighbors. Did we ever have a problem? I bought your house trying to help you out and what happens to Doug? Your enemies burn my house down. You know me. Nobody is after old Douglas Patterson. Most likely, someone is after you!"

Monica felt her heart sink as he spoke his peace. Paula was also tense, knowing that her partner had scored some mighty big blows against organized crime.

Mr. Patterson says, "Go talk to Chuck Ferline. His boys were at Dudley Field. They can tell you what the stranger looked like."

They said their good byes.

The women followed through on the lead. Chuck and the boys discussed the appearance of the plane operator. The man was husky, had a deep voice, and the boys would know him if they saw him again.

The agents asked Chuck if the boys would help by looking at some photos. They agreed to meet on the weekend.

After parting company, they discussed the next moves.

They rode to Dudley Field. It was a large recreation park with baseball fields. There was a swimming pool, but it was far from the field where the model plane was located. The agents asked neighbors if they saw anything that fateful day. They didn't get any new leads.

Chicago

A few days later outside of Chicago at the godfather's villa the error is discussed.

"Boris, a mistake has been made. You'll have to go back to Ohio. The bitch moved. She lives in Fairport Harbor now. My cousin, Sal Cambello, found out. You guys nose around the town. We ain't through. You and Lou need to try again. This woman is like a cat. She got nine lives. Maybe only eight now, so let's take this bitch down."

Chapter 11
Watch List and Stern's Baby

Brenda Clark supplied a little information about Palmino Franco after her first meeting with Attorney Dom DeLargo. It turned into an affair. She enjoyed his company because he made her feel young.

Feeling confident, she rattled off some minor detail about Franco's casino. The junior attorney acted very impressed and assured her the Columbus casino committee would be receptive to Franco's casino idea if she gave a speech outlining the casino plan.

Her error in judgment came soon after a romp in the sack with the young attorney. Taking a timeout, Brenda looked in her purse. As she relaxed, she pulled out a confidential pink list of Franco's staff. People hired or being recruited made the list. She mentioned the list as a passing thought.

Something was added to the list that Brenda didn't know. A bogus name was on the list. She was an Oregon celebrity. The name was a Franco plant, an imposter. Mr. Franco intentionally gave Brenda the false information as a test. Brenda thought she had an exclusive copy of Mr. Franco's inner circle.

She overconfidently said, "You keep up this intensity and I'll help you meet Mr. Franco's inner circle. He has some rich donors, who are close Las Vegas friends. They're ready to assist in making the casino a reality."

She was lying. Although the list did contain staff members and their future duties, there wasn't a Las Vegas connection that she could positively identify, nor did Franco mention any rich donors.

Normally, Brenda guarded her purse but when she went to the bathroom she left it sitting on the night stand. Mr. DeLargo pulled the pink paper from her purse and used his cell phone to photograph the list.

Simone Porter, Brenda Clark, Dallas Young, John Pfefferkorn, Quentin Piotrowski, Cindy Avalon, Catlin Wise, Tammy Wysocki, and Brian Bard were names on the list.

Brenda referenced Simone Porter often, so the junior attorney already knew her. Some listed people were already on Mr. Franco's staff and others had peripheral knowledge of the building going on in Lake County.

Cindy Avalon was recruited from Las Vegas to be his Master of Ceremony, hostess, and she was an actress. She often played the role of a Princess in Franco's Oregon casino shows. Catlin Wise, the artist, was to operate Franco's visual aids and publicity department. Oregon lodge owner, Tammy Wysocki and her staff would operate the log cabin resort which was part of Franco's winter amusement park, if he could persuade her to leave the fishing camp in Oregon for a few months. Food distribution was Mr. Piotrowski's specialty. He and Wysocki's staff would double team the food service business for sports tournaments. Young and Pfefferkorn were in charge of security. Brian Bard, a wrestling coach, was a sports specialist. He was into big time wrestling, which was going to be another winter attraction.

After Mrs. Clark and DeLargo went there separate ways, DeLargo headed for an early meeting with his senior member of the casino committee.

An advisor to the governor, Devlin Culliver asks, "Does Palmino Franco really intend to build a hotel and casino in Lake County? This is very risky. Folks nothing has been approved. The people haven't passed a casino issue. Why are we jumping the gun?"

Three Months Later

Franco was pressing ahead and this made government politicians nervous. The Ohio lottery was a sacred money making machine, a cash cow. Senior politicians started to worry about the casino threat as did the syndicate.

The seriousness of the situation was turning heads. A race track owner, a Cleveland developer, and a rich Cleveland politician called the governor to demand the proposed building be stopped. Their message was simple. Lake County can't have a casino. Others have the right before an outsider is allowed.

Attorney Sean Joseph was adamant, "If he's building a casino, it has to stop. Our friends in Cleveland, Detroit, and Las Vegas have donated money to our casino campaign. The casino committee has an obligation, an understanding, that only Cleveland, Toledo, Columbus and Cincinnati will be receiving authorization for a casino. Who does Palmino Franco think he is?"

Brenda Clark was called back to Columbus. She hustled south to calm the big shots. She made it known that the hotel was being built first. A casino grand opening would come later if approved. While her first meeting was low level, it was enough to cause the sabers to be drawn. Tension was pulling on the political vine. The first crack appearing in the casino discussion was forming.

A second hastily arranged meeting was organized when a newspaper article claimed that an Oregon casino owner/operator was interested in building a hotel in Lake County. This news hit home because he wasn't just interested; he was building a hotel and casino.

Some political folks in Columbus were generally rattled by the news. Brenda Clark had to meet with the governor's people to explain. She was clever to mention the fact that Ohio gamblers were taking money out of Ohio and leaving the cash in border states. For this reason an Ohio casino made sense. Franco was building a private casino. It wouldn't cost the taxpayers a dime. Since only four casinos were proposed for

Ohio, why not add a fifth casino? The best casino managers will get the business. Mr. Franco never said it would open as a casino. It would be a sports park and offer casino gambling if approved. It would just be built ahead of schedule. In closing Mrs. Clark said Franco was a man who got things done. He liked to be first.

She ended the meeting with two questions. "Gentleman, do you want Northern Ohio to succeed and become a tourist haven?"

Richard received a text message from Brenda saying that she left town for Columbus in a hurry. She wouldn't be back for a few days. Richard Stern had some breathing room. When the cat is away the mouse will play. Stern's off and on conviction to not drink started to drift. Moving away from resolute abstinence, he shed the role of teetotaler.

With Brenda gone, the leash was off the dog. It meant conditions were perfect for a relapse. Stern wasn't helping himself. With beer on his mind abstention was fading fast. He was planning on a visit to the Redi Go convenience store.

One mistake nearly every alcoholic makes is consuming the first drink. All the others don't matter. It happened. After two days of heavy drinking, Stern knew two things. One, he shouldn't have started drinking. Two, he should stop, but wouldn't or couldn't.

On the third day of binge drinking his nerves were frayed. Stern paced the kitchen floor. The pain of withdrawal from alcohol was real. He knew if he had one shot or beer the craving would subside. His body yearned for medicine. One drink was all he needed. The mental agony would miraculously vanish with a drink, but only to be replaced with false hope. He decided; he'll just have one. Subconsciously, his mind plays him like a fiddle.

Down the hatch goes the first one. Stern's lie was cast a thousand times. Every alcoholic says the same thing. He knew what he should do. Will power was lacking, but it was needed.

"I should call, Dave Skytta or maybe Father Pete. No, no, too much bother, I can handle this. Hell, I'm sick, I need medicine. I'll just have one. I'm going to get better. I know the ropes."

Submission, Stern slowly gives in. He opens the refrigerator door. The last Shorts is standing tall. A sixteen ounce beer is in there. It is neatly tucked away, a reserve, a medic in a can. Even if it is only temporary relief, Stern says that it will be worth it. Closer he edges to the refrigerator shelf. He triumphantly gives himself permission. Richard's subconscious toys with him. The moment of truth is tolling. He reaches in and grabs the beer can.

As if ashamed, he walks to the phone next to the kitchen nook to call his friend only one block down the road. He needs help, but his fingernail is under the tab.

"Pop," the tab bursts open the can.

The temptation is too great. He chugs down one third. Sets the beer can down and puts his shoes on. Two more gulps and another third makes him feel a little better.

This occasion was no different than any other for Stern. He found some instant relief from the can of beer. He had another reason to be less concerned about his self-control because his bank account was soaring from the reward money he received from the FBI. For helping bust a ring of terrorists, he had well over a hundred thousand, a jumbo, in one bank account.

"This one beer isn't going to do it. Road trip, I say."

Richard grabs his coat and out the door he goes. He drives to High Street and stops at the Redi-Go convenience store. Woody Jedlicka, one of the store owners, waves at Stern.

As he walks through the store, two girls are shifting a baby between each other. Stern remembers seeing the girls, Rachel Jeavons and Taylor Landies in a high school play. They're showing off the baby. Rachel and Taylor are surrounded by patrons and counter help. Woody walks over to get his two cents in. Another store patron, Donna Schindler calls to bank manager Katy Childress to look. Soon they're joined by Laura, the bank teller.

Woody asks Katy, "Who's at the bank?"

Katy has a quick answer.

"Woody, it's Wednesday afternoon, we just closed."

Rachel says, "Monica Micovich is our new neighbor. This is her son, Michael. Its Monica's first. She let me and Taylor take him out for a ride. Isn't he adorable, little Michael Micovich?"

Upon hearing Rachel speak about the baby and Monica, Stern's ears went up like an antenna. He almost skidded on the floor as he abruptly stopped his march to the beer cooler. He did an abound face knowing that the baby, little Michael, might be his son.

Richard Stern had a flashback to the month he and Monica had an enchanting evening. Even though he was quite drunk that evening he remembered the moment. He did it. Knowing how embarrassing it was for Monica, he promised to never say a word about the affair. He counted the months on his fingers. Over and over he counted. He didn't dare say anything as he tried to peer over the huddled mass. When he saw the baby, Richard's eyes started to well with tears of joy. He was overcome. It was God's gift, but he couldn't be sure. He just knew he was the father.

After a mesmerizing minute, Stern realized people were starting to filter away. Katy and Donna, the two bank employees, saw Mr. Stern.

"Hi, Mr. Stern. Isn't he a beautiful baby, Mr. Stern?" questions Katy.

"Oh, yah; almost looks like me when I was a baby," confesses Richard.

"Nice looking baby, girls!" Richard says to the babysitter and then he asks, "Monica Micovich, that name rings a bell. Does she live in town?"

"Yes! Do you know Miss Micovich?"

Stern was petrified by the question. He looked at the babysitter and then looked down at the baby. Sheepishly, he answers in a half truth.

"Well, yah, I'm somewhat sure we crossed paths at some point in time."

Richard raced to the cooler and plucked out a twelve pack. He adds a six pack of malt liquor to his load. The baby was cause for celebration.

Stern is about to pay at the counter.

"Add eight cigars, Renee. I'm going to celebrate."

He pays the cashier and drives home. Once inside his house he rejoices.

"God, I'm going to quit drinking and be a father. Somehow, I'm going to get visitation rights. Right now, I just have to party a little bit. Michael Micovich Stern, I'm going to help you grow. You're not going to be a drunk. No, not like me, I'm going to get better. I want you to be a great man. I hope you like baseball."

Richard thought about the promise he made to Monica. He wondered. Where does Monica live? He would never interfere with her life, but somehow, he has to be a part of Michael's life.

"I've got to help her."

Richard looks at his cats and says, "Boots, you and Shorts hold down the fort. I've got to share the news. I think I'm a father."

Jumping for joy, Richard raced to the bar with the fantastic news. He truly believes he is the father even though he has no positive proof. He keeps repeating.

"I promised Monica that I would never reveal the affair."

The alcohol was weighing on his mind. His big mouth was about to open Pandora's Box.

Chapter 12
Bar Talk

The exulted father didn't waste time racing to his tavern. After all that he witnessed, he had reason to celebrate. Not that he needed a reason for drinking, he didn't. His party mood was merely reinforced by the fact that he might be a father. In reality this was only an excuse. A drop of a hat would have been enough to start Stern off on another binge.

Just before he entered the tavern, he took time to bring himself down to earth. The shock from seeing his son was a high point in his life. Although he wasn't entirely sure the baby was his, he had pretty good reason to believe he was the father. He wondered if he should call Agent Paula or maybe Cliff Moses. No, he couldn't call the FBI chief. Cliff would get angry if he were to interfere in Monica's life. He had Paula's phone number. Maybe the girls in the bar would offer some suggestions as to how he could find out for sure if Michael was truly his son. As usual Stern decided to have a few drinks and think about the dilemma.

Sitting at the bar Richard engaged in small talk. He gulped a beer waiting for the perfect moment to break the news. Having a shot now and then between the beers, he started to loosen up. His talk was starting to flow freely. Thinking about the promise he made to Monica, (he would never say anything about their affair) he was having a bout of loose lips. He makes a desperation play at holding his tongue.

Richard comments, "Andy, I'm going outside for a little fresh air. I have something important to tell you, but I swore to keep a secret."

Stern wanted to cool down. If he spilled the beans, he'd be breaking a promise, so he walked to his van to think about it. Once inside he picked up his cell phone and dialed Paula Gavalia's phone number.

"Hello, Paula, it's Stern, Richard Stern. I'll bet you're surprised to hear from the master of disguises."

"Mr. Stern, you're a legend with the FBI. Are you OK?"

The reaction was typical Paula. Her first thought was that he was drinking. She wanted Mr. Stern to get his life on track.

"Yes, I'm OK."

Richard knew how caring she was. Although she was a crime fighter, she was a compassionate person.

"Paula, I have a serious question to ask."

"I like serious questions; go for it, Mr. Stern."

"OK, but this question is a tough one," says the hesitant ex-FBI informer.

Paula answers, "Yes, Mr. Stern, I like tough questions, spit it out."

"There's a convenience store in Fairport. It's called the Redi Go Food Mart and I saw a baby in there. Not just any baby mind you. The babysitter, who was carting this young baby around, said that it's Monica Micovich's son, Michael. I overheard her say Monica and Michael just moved to Fairport and they're neighbors. I've seen the babysitter at a house on New Street. After I added two and two together, I wondered. I think, I, I, oh, holy mackerel. Am I the father of Michael?"

The phone went silent. Stern held his cell phone tight to his ear waiting for an answer. Silence, he waited and waited. Richard was bracing for an answer. Judging by the silence, he knew the answer. He was indeed, the father.

"Holy mackerel, Paula! It's true; isn't it? He's my son! I can be a good father."

Almost admonishing himself of his past affair, Stern let her know he wanted to be involved with the son.

Paula wouldn't lie. Time for fending off the question was buried by Richard's hysteria. He was singing praise and then his voice turned serious, but she could tell he was overjoyed. She turned on a more personal interjection.

"Richard, you're the father. You mustn't say a word to anyone. Do you understand, Richard?"

Stern, looking at the blinking beer sign in the tavern window, knows full well what he's about to do.

Richard asks, "Did she tell you? Did she tell you I'm the father?"

"Yes, Richard."

"Holy mackerel, surprise, surprise, I'm a dad! I'm going to quit drinking, no swearing, and no cigars after tonight, Paula."

Agent Gavalia says, "That would be steps in the right direction. Can you keep this a secret, Richard? You have to promise."

Richard crossed his fingers as he answered.

"Oh, the secret is buried. You don't have to worry about me, Paula. My lips are sealed. Thanks for letting me know. I'll sleep much better now."

"Fine, good bye, dad," says Paula as she hangs up the phone.

Happier then a pig in mud, he dashed back into the tavern. Stern's mind worked to find the perfect place to blurt out the words. Struggling, trying to hold back the news and listening, he fought back the urge to say what was dancing in his mind. For sure he didn't want to give up Monica's name. Although this was a sworn secret, the booze was freeing his tongue, like a crowbar extracting a tightly held nail.

Mel and Andy were talking about kids and sports. Their kids were out of high school. Andy's voice was starting to carry across the room as he smacked his lips after hoisting a shot of scotch. Upon entering the conversation at that moment, Stern ordered another shot of Cuddy for his buddy, Andy and a beer for Mel. All three were mellow.

Andy proclaimed, "Today, kids have much better sport's equipment then we had. Golf clubs, softball and baseball bats are way better. What's it going to be like for the next generation? Tell me, Richard. What's the next generation going to play?

The question was perfectly timed. Intoxicated, his voice carried a note of mild treason. In a way Stern turned into Judas. Truth and a lie in one sentence were ready. Finally, he couldn't hold back any longer. Richard studied the group. As if the last domino was set, his finger was on the talk button. The booze had done its job.

He opened up. "Everyone, I have a little surprise to share."

Only a couple people were sitting off to the end of the bar. A big man, Boris, who introduced himself to Whitney, the waitress, was drinking his third straight vodka. The other man was Boris' friend, Louie Looma. Louie, a pudgy fellow, was keeping an eye on Boris. This was because the godfather didn't have much faith in Boris. Then again, Louis didn't have an iron-clad past. The two men got along well together because they shared a troubled past and similar taste for fine dining.

The other patrons and employees were massed around Stern as if he was master of ceremony. Stern's faithful drinking buddies, Andy and Mel, were all ears when he broke the news. The crowd moved close.

Stern used two fingers from each hand to hold out a cigar with the wrapper displaying the sign 'It's a boy.'

"I'm a father! Just call me DAD. I just found out my old girlfriend had a baby. It turns out the little guy is my child. The mother and my son moved into town. I saw my son at the Redi Go Food Mart. Can you believe this?"

The booze had sanctioned the statements flowing from his lips.

The term 'girlfriend' was completely off the mark. It didn't matter. Stern was in his glory. He said it and now was prepared to unleash a barrage of mendacities. The antonymic flow was about to begin.

"Now this wasn't a lasting love affair. I mean, we did share intimate moments. She cared for me. Her friend, Paula, she's an FBI agent too. I keep in touch with her."

He blabbed just like he said he wouldn't. The booze got the better or worst of him. He couldn't stop now. He ordered a round for the house. As he handed out cigars to those that wanted them, more questions followed.

Mel asks, "Who's the mother? Do we know her, Richard?

Whitney chipped in, "Who is it, Richard?"

"That's a secret. I don't want to say anything more."

Whitney asks. "Come on, Richard, who is the mother? Is she really a FBI agent?"

"It might be Monica Micovich, Debbie Kennedy, or Paula Gavalia that's all I'm saying. It might not be any of those girls. Only God knows and you don't need to know anything more. Don't you guys know how easy it is for gossip to start flowing in Fairport Harbor?"

Anita says, "We'll find out, Richard. You can't keep that a secret."

"I'm protecting her identity," says Richard.

Dumbfounded, Boris and Louie stared at each other after hearing the bar talk.

The buzz was stirring in the tavern. The waitresses gathered to hash over the news. Stern ventured to the restroom, followed by Boris Gedeon.

As they finished washing their hands, Boris candidly says he can help Mr. Stern's love life. The flowers shop he owns has a nice way of saying hello to a lost love.

Boris says, "The girl you dated, it's Monica Micovich. I know her. We've sold flowers to her. She's a nice woman. You need a nice way of saying, welcome to Fairport Harbor."

Mr. Stern turned to look at the big man.

"How do you know?" Mr. Stern asks.

"You gave me a free cigar and I've been listening to you talk. I'm in the business of building love and friendship. I'm in the flower business. Keep this idea a secret. I'm going to fix you up with a nice gift for her. We'll send her some flowers with your initials on the package. You can repay me if it works and I know it will. The next time you see me, well, let's just say you'll be filled with emotion. Love, say it with flowers, buddy," says Boris.

Once again the feeling of exultation grips him. Clearly intoxicated, Mr. Stern is presented with an indirect opportunity to say something nice to the girl he loves and the one he offended in the past.

He slaps the man on the shoulder.

Stern says, "That's a good idea, thanks, friend," as he walks from the restroom.

Chapter 13
Norton Otis OK

Living two houses away from Monica was mean and miserable Norton Otis. Retired from the F-P and E railroad, the old man hunted rabbits for food. The past time sport was getting the best of Otis. For one thing, Mr. Otis was a bad shot. The beagle he hunted with kept him company, but Otis never treated the dog very well. The kids around the neighborhood would play with his pet which seemed to irk Otis. Otis Norton's dog was a good hunter, but like Otis the best days were gone and the dog finally passed.

The dog was buried in the back yard. Hardly grieving, wasting little time, Otis went to the animal shelter for another companion.

What was Otis looking for? He wanted a cost effective hunter. So he made a miserable choice, choosing a big dog, which wasn't a pure beagle. Not the great hunter the folks at the animal shelter made him out to be, Otis became frustrated when the dog failed to perform like his old dog. After three tries Norton Otis turned mean and scolded the dog.

"I thought you were a hunting dog, you lousy mutt," shouted Mr. Otis.

"Out you go. Now you'll have to learn how to hunt. Find your own food," yelled the cranky old man. Driving away as he pushed the dog out the passenger window, Otis felt no remorse. He abandoned the dog.

Monica noticed that Norton Otis didn't have a dog with him as he usually does. She remembered him saying something to the dog when she saw them a couple days ago. The dog she saw in his backyard looked like an oversized beagle.

Monica had a ham bone that would make a tasty toy for the dog. She walked over to Mr. Otis's driveway as he was getting out of the station wagon.

"Hello, sir, I'm your neighbor a couple houses down the street."

"Yeah, I saw you moving in. What do you want?"

Monica was surprised by his feisty attitude. She chocked it up to old age and loneliness.

Monica says, "I have a hambone for your dog. I heard you say his name, OK"

Norton Otis answers sharply, "His name was OK, but he ain't OK. I give him back from where he came. He couldn't hunt rabbits like Spike, my other dog. You won't see him around here. OK is gone. I'll get another dog. Keep your bone, lady. Go make some bean soup."

That was enough for Monica. She turned around and marched back to her home.

OK ran into the bushes near the lake after his master sped away. OK found a female friend near the lake. They splash around until the owner called for his dog. She dashed off leaving OK to ponder his next move.

Although young, the dog wasn't stupid. OK worked his way down the shoreline until night fall.

Night time was a different matter as OK had a close encounter with a skunk. It wasn't a fair exchange as far as OK could determine. He'd have a difficult time hiding from strangers by the way he smelled. Sadly, OK started to realize that he was on his own. He passed through the backyard of the West property and made his way to Prospect Street. He traveled down the beach road and made his way to the bottom of the lighthouse hill. Doubling back to the beach, it was getting late.

Chapter 14
Rescued by OK

Leaving his tavern without saying goodbye was typical Stern drama. Stern sent a two word text message tipping off the manager. **Good night** was on Anita's cell phone. She knew Mr. Stern was completely intoxicated. She really didn't want him around the bar when he was in such bad shape, so the message was welcome news.

Once outside the tavern the midnight air was enough to revive Mr. Stern. He didn't dare drive home. If there was a rule Stern found sacred, it was no drinking and driving. He grabbed his coat from the van and stuffed the van keys in his zippered coat pocket. The coat contained a surprise. Inside the breast pocket Stern had hid a stainless steel flask of black-berry brandy. The medicine was perfectly stowed away. Using leg power, he started walking. Lake Erie wasn't far away. At a fast pace he broke into a snaking trot. Passing down Second Street he turned right on Vine Street until he came to Prospect Street.

Stern was prepared to spend a little time with the night critters. He pulled the brandy out of the coat for a booster shot. Not just one, he had to have a second helping.

Taking care to stow the medicine, a memory flashed in his mind. His cousin, Frank and brother Jim hid out of sight over the bank. Here, they smoked cigarettes as mischievous youngsters.

The spot where he was standing was a makeshift driving range. Stern got his first golfing lessons from the man who owned the house on the corner. He used to teach him how to drive a golf ball from the top of the bank to the water. John was the golf pro at the Honey Hole Club.

Sticks lying on the ground reminded him of golf clubs and the driving lessons. Reaching down he found a suitable imitation of a golf club. After taking a couple practice swings to loosen up; Stern coiled like a spring. The release wasn't well timed as the ground gave way under his feet. It was too late to recover. Trying to gain balance he started sliding. First on his butt, then he hit a small log that didn't give. Catapulting forward, the next move was a summersault sending him airborne. Hands extended, the drunken airborne body was flexible enough to absorb the first bounce. His head glanced off the tree at the bottom of the bank, until he flattened out on the road at the bottom of the bank.

Out for a moment, Stern was unconscious. His vision was blurred. He leaped to his feet and stood still for a moment. His legs were wobbly. Looking up where he was just a few seconds before, he felt a trickle of blood passing over his eyebrow. A slight wound on his forehead was starting to form a bump.

The water washing on the shore wasn't that far away so Stern walked across the road to the beach. As he squatted down at the shore to splash water on his face, he started to faint. Falling forward into the water again, he made a desperate attempt to save himself. This time the water doused the sleeves on his shirt as his arms buckled. Fear penetrated his soul as he felt hopelessly weak. His head became a millstone.

Helpless, almost drowning on the shore, he called out.

"Help," cried Stern. The silence didn't leave him much hope. He was so intoxicated and dizzy; he thought the end was near. Again, pushing up he could barely get his face out of the water. The drunken state and concussion sapped his coordination and strength.

Behind him, Stern heard a movement, a rustle, and then a splash indicating someone was almost next to him. He reached out.

"Help!" Stern managed a look under his armpit using the moonlight as an aid; he could see a dog. He tried to hold out his arm, but fell on his elbow. Again he tried.

"Help me, boy," cried Stern.

Splashing into the water, the dog moved in front of Stern. Miraculously, the dog grabbed Mr. Stern's sleeve and pulled him. Richard aided the rescue by holding around the back of the dogs head. The strength of the dog helped spin Stern around so that his face was out of the water.

Stern passed out.

The dog sat with Richard Stern for the next three hours. He watched until Mr. Stern revived. As Stern looked at the dog he remembered the rescue. At that moment the dog sensed the man was OK. He ran toward the brick building, a beach refreshment stand, stopped for a moment, and looked back. The dog then bolted across the sandy street. Up the bank he ran.

Stern moved to the beach to escape the water's edge. Still groggy, he shut his eyes for what seemed like a minute. In reality he was out for another hour.

Clouds started to cover the moon. Only the street light down the road lit up the snack stand. The wind off Lake Erie was only a mild breeze. Off to the west the fog horn at the lighthouse gave out an audible blare.

Richard rose off the ground. He was cold, wet, but alive because of the dog.

Shaking from the cool morning breeze, he started to walk home. The body was functioning, although he had a slight headache and he felt a bump on his forehead.

It was still dark outside. The streetlight illuminated his way. The trek up Prospect Hill that led to the beach wasn't as much fun as it used to be when he was a child. The hill was only a block away from his deceased parent's house. Something about the walk was familiar as he came to the top of the hill. How miserably strange the walk is.

Being semi-drunk, cold, and alone was a major difference from the old days. Stern's old stumping ground didn't grow old. The hill, once a sled riding paradise as a youth, became a hill of pain for the middle-aged business owner.

Hightailing out of the brush was a cotton-tail rabbit. The white flash of the bunny's tail was followed by another white flash. A dog passed by almost ten yards behind the bunny.

Not sprinting, but moving along at a good pace, the mixed breed dog must've had beagle in his line as his nose was on the scent. He stopped for a moment, perhaps to take a look at the man he saved.

Mr. Stern had no way of thanking the stocky dog. He could only pray that the rabbit made to his hole and hope the dog would find his master. Little did Stern know that the dog was an orphan? His master abandoned him. Only concerned with getting home without being seen, Richard was embarrassed by the ordeal of the last night. Fortunately, the trek home wasn't that far.

When he arrived at home, he tried to collect his thoughts. The booze did it again. Remembering that he spouted off in the tavern and being saved from drowning by a dog, Stern felt remorseful. No longer could he afford to act like a reckless, young stud. He was a father.

"I'm going to quit drinking." said Stern. I have to find a way."

Sadly, it was a statement said many times.

Chapter 15
Creaky Step

The annual Marti Gras parade marched through town which was well attended by folks young and old. The entire town of Fairport Harbor seemed to come alive. Monica and Paula walked around the town before the parade. They were amazed by the size of the crowd. Car loads of people were coming into town.

They settled on Seventh Street to watch the parade. The parade wouldn't start for an hour, but the street was filling up. As Paula readied her camera she spotted a couple of men in a new Cadillac followed by an antique police van. The well dressed men in the caddy appeared out of place. She snapped two pictures of the cars as they drove by. The cigar smoking passengers reminded her of 1930's mobsters. She thought it was part of the parade. Paula nudged Monica.

Paula says, "Looks like Al Capone is back." Monica agreed. They didn't know how close to right they were.

Mr. Franco hired a team of float designers to market the casino idea for the parade. He was softening up the local crowd by advancing the casino idea and being creative. Some Fairport Harbor residents from Chestnut Street used their talent to construct a giant house of cards float. Franco was very pleased with their work. The two floats were complimented by art work from The Pencil Box Company.

The parade started the long weekend and it was followed by three days of celebration at the beach park. A fireworks display cemented the last day of the event. The festival passed without any problems. It was a sign that summer was in full swing.

The Independence Day holiday interrupted the Harbor Construction crew. They worked for a couple days, followed by a few days off. Work resumed, the pounding went on for two weeks.

Every so often Mr. Babb would check on the progress. Almost daily Monica would stroll with the baby and glance through the window to check on the workers. They were doing a methodical job, working on the windows, floor boards in the hall and kitchen, but seem to be held up by the work on the steps. Monica noticed some frustration on the part of the foreman. She overheard the foreman lambasting one of the carpenters.

Harry says, "Hank, you're a fat ass. The steps are telling you that. There's no noise when I go up the steps."

After two weeks nearly all the carpentry was finished except for one step leading upstairs. A creaky step gave them fits. A noise played a vanishing act, intermittently sounding out when a heavy person got near the final upstairs steps. The creak seemed to move every time they thought they had the problem resolved. They resorted to using shims and screws to batten down the problem.

Finally, the construction crew pronounced the mysterious creak fixed. The workers fought through the problems. All was cured. The trial and error method eliminated nearly every problem they could find. Monica was pleased by their effort to tracking down every loose board. Even the attic stairs received some attention. The job was quite a task.

Steve Babb received a report from the foreman. Harry said that a couple windows were replaced in the baby's room, a back door was replaced, and new locks installed. The pesky problems were the steps going upstairs. They were pronounced repaired as well as the hallway and kitchen creaks. Harry had the itemized list of repairs which he handed over to Mr. Babb.

Watching the workers file out with trash and tools, Monica knew the job was complete. When she got the call from Mr. Babb, she was relieved. He would meet with her to go over the final inspection.

As she pushed Michael along in the stroller, Mr. Babb pulled up in the company car. Monica was glad to get the job done.

They went over the costs. Everything was in order. During his explanation, Monica noted an added piece of advice.

Speaking about the creaky floor boards, he says, "Monica, the problems are all eliminated. One step going upstairs was a real nightmare. I thought my guys would never find the creak. The foreman said 'only a very heavy person could set off the creak,' but he thinks it's gone forever. We're pretty confident all the noise has been eliminated."

With a smile on her face, Monica says, "I think I overheard him say that."

Chapter 16
Phone Call

Paula sat nervously thinking out loud. Hoping, wishing she could believe Mr. Stern. Sharing a secret with him was not a good idea, especially if he'd been drinking.

"He's going to say something about Monica. He's going to say 'I love her.'"

Paula begins to think out loud. She should call Mr. Stern and tell him another secret that has been on her mind.

"I can't say; 'Mr. Stern, Monica does care about you.' That's asking for trouble."

She couldn't tell him that. But, she thought, it's true. Certainly, she would never say to her partner something she would immediately deny.

Pretending to talk into the phone, Paula says, "Monica, you and Richard might make a nice couple."

When she thought about Monica's comment on a late night stakeout, she became spellbound. Monica mentioned that she overheard Stern say he had another child from a previous marriage and he wants another.

At the time Monica said that Stern was plenty drunk, so she cast off the dispersion.

Engrossed, Paula says, "Stern does this kind of stuff; he's psychic."

As an informer for the FBI, Stern's track record presented a clear picture for Paula since she worked with him. Uncanny accusations being his trademark, he was telling the truth most of the time, not that he had any reason to lie. This fact made her more fidgety.

Being the bodyguard for Stern was like cranking a jack in the box or spinning a the cylinder of a loaded gun. He could be fun or something could go wrong unexpectedly. Yet, he was friendly and good natured most of the time. Stern managed to get into jams no matter how many agents were deployed.

"I wish I never would have said anything to him" says Paula.

Most likely she thought, he'll get drunk and shoot his mouth off. Should she call her boss with the news? She kept wondering, hesitating, and coiling her hair around her index finger. It was a delaying tactic. Should she call Cliff and leave a message?

"No, he's away on vacation!"

Her friend was the biggest concern.

First things first, she had to tell Monica. She pushed the numbers for Monica's cell phone. Feeling tense, her heart was pounding. She listened for the receiver to make the connection.

After five rings, Monica answered the phone after viewing the incoming phone number.

"Hi, partner," says Monica.

"Hi, Monica, I, ah, I've got interesting news, ah, kind of big news for you. Maybe something you might not want to hear."

Her words would normally flow in order. This hesitation tipped off Monica. Together with the sound of her voice meant she was stressed.

"Oh, oh, sounds like trouble. What's up?"

Paula says, "You better sit down if you're standing."

"Gee, Paula, come on, what's wrong?"

"Well. Are you sitting down?"

"Yes, tell me. Please!"

Paula let it fly.

"Richard Stern called me."

Monica says, "Richard Stern called you; Stern called you! Well let's see, a first guess, he knows about Michael doesn't he? You told him, didn't you?"

Paula didn't realize her friend was going to throw it back in her face. They both waited as if a no talking contest was in progress.

The pause was long enough for Paula to realize she better say something. The news must have sunk in. She could almost envision Monica's facial expression.

Monica sat silent. The day was upon her. She was in a semi-state of shock, but knew the day would come when Stern would find out that he was the father.

Monica resolved her misconception. The misfired romance with Bill Wright and search for a suitable father was over. She's living in Fairport Harbor now and the day would come when Michael would ask about his dad. She wanted to say something good.

Her past dealings with Richard were an adventure. She already contemplated putting rules in place. Stern could have visitation provided he was sober. Monica and Paula already agreed that he wasn't a bad guy, just a man with an identity problem and an alcoholic. He was a fun guy to be around. He wasn't a boring guy.

Paula says, "You know I didn't just tell him outright."

Monica asks, "What did you tell him?"

"Well, he said he saw a baby at the store, the one by the bank. I think, maybe the Redi Go Food Mart. The babysitter was showing off the baby. Richard overheard the babysitter saying that Monica Micovich is the mother. It registered for Mr. Stern. Then he called and asked me if I knew who the father was. I told him the truth."

Monica expressed the inevitable to her partner.

"Oh my God! Taylor and Rachel took Michael for a walk. They must have stopped at Woody's convenience store."

Paula, apologetically says, "I'm sorry, I couldn't lie."

"It's ok, Paula. I'll deal with it. I'm not going to run around pretending he's not the father. After what Bill did, well, I'm through with him. Bill seemed like he would be a good father figure, but I found out the hard way. Bill Wright is a two-timer and Stern is the legitimate father. He'll have to get his act together if he wants to see his son."

Surprised by Monica's restraint, Paula comments, "You obviously thought about this. I'm really proud of you, Monica. Such restraint, you're remarkable."

Monica says, "Save it, Paula. Stern will have to get off the booze."

Paula says, "Richard could be a good father."

Monica says, "I don't know. Richard has a long way to go before he becomes Mr. Dad. I mean, he could get better. I know he's not all that bad."

Paula says, "Well, you must have thought, maybe you can change him."

"Do you think I slept with him to get him off the booze?"

Paula answers, "No, never mind, forget it."

"Tell me, Paula. What are you thinking?"

"Cliff was really proud of you when you saved Richard's life. Maybe you were falling for him when you saved his life."

"What are you saying?"

Paula tries to explain. She believes Monica might want more than just a friendship from Richard. The words started to flow.

"Let me finish. I'm your friend, so don't get mad. Maybe deep down that's why you slept with him. He obviously wanted you and maybe you needed him right then," says Paula.

"You know better than that. Good bye, Paula, Michael says good bye, too."

"I'm sorry. I didn't mean you're in love with him, but ah, ah. Bye, Monica, Don't be mad. I just thought that maybe."

Monica, somewhat distraught by the supposition, heard enough. While she didn't want her partner advancing such a notion, there was truth in her words. Monica held a soft spot for Richard. A deep inner secret, one her partner recognized, but she didn't dare tell, not even her friend. Richard was an older man. She wondered what it was she saw.

"It's ok, Paula, we're friends. Thanks for sharing your thoughts. Bye.

Monica's father was much like Mr. Stern. He was adventurous, never afraid to make a mistake, and he had a heart of gold.

Paula sat by the phone reflecting on the conversation. So nerve wracking was the ordeal, she twisted a knot in her hair.

Recalling the life and death ordeal, when they were on the Eastlake party boat, the Ranger, she shivered. Immediately following the shooting, Paula watched Monica come to Mr. Stern's aid when he was wounded. She could see there was more between Monica and Richard.

Monica sat with her elbows on the table. She remembered the situation with the passengers on the boat and she remembered how Mr. Stern surprised the terrorists. After the shooting, she was emotional as she held him; hoping and praying he was ok.

Chapter 17
Kidnap a Baby

"I'm not for this, Boris. You missed your opportunity. You start messing with a mother's baby, well, I'm not for this."

Boris replies, "The boss says we missed an opportunity. You got it. We missed an opportunity. We got to teach her a lesson. I got a new plan started. Do you remember the guy yesterday handing out cigars, the father, the drunk in the bar?"

Lou says, "Yah, what about him?"

"He thinks flowers are being sent to Monica Micovich to warm her heart. The flowers are the perfect bouquet to case out the house. You can deliver the flowers.

"Me? You want me to deliver flowers?"

"Yah, aren't we nice guys?"

Lou says, "Oh, yah, we're nice guys all right. Let's not do this."

Boris says, "What're you yellow? You have to make a delivery. That's all."

"Oh, man, I don't like this. You're going to get us in trouble, Boris."

Boris says, "We need to case out the house."

Lou had another idea, but the godfather would have to give the final order.

"If you really want to fix her, I know a couple who could do this job. Let's use them. I'm not going to kidnap a baby. I can cook the books, deal from the bottom of the deck, but I'm not going to take a kid," says Lou.

"Don't worry, Lou. My plan is to put a little scare into her. What I really need is a sacrificial lamb. We need somebody to take the wrap."

Lou says, "Oh man, you're going to burn the help."

Lou looks up at the sky, "Jesus, he doesn't know what he's doing."

He turns to Boris, "You're a rotten cutthroat."

"Thanks, Lou." Boris asks, "OK, now that you know me, who do you know that wants to make some cold cash? We need a couple of risk takers."

Lou asks, "Are you going to pay?

Boris points to a suitcase in the van.

"Look, I got money, lots of cash. The boss wants this job done. Come now, my friend. Would I cheat?" Boris asks.

"Christ, do I have to answer," says Lou.

The Russian born mobster had a bag of tricks to use. He partially opened the suitcase sitting on the floor of the van. A layer of real money was on top and the rest was fake money. Boris had already skimmed away most of the real loot for himself; left was pay for the hired help. Boris fully opened the suitcase of hundred dollar bills. The money looked real.

"Aren't you worried about my friends stealing the cash without doing the job?

The question Lou asked was a legitimate one.

Lou says, "Well, if you burn them, I don't care. These two are lower than you, Boris."

Boris replies, "If they screw up, they can make a sacrifice for all the bad they've done."

Lou says, "Christ, you're going to burn them. I just know it. Well, that's ok. This couple, their bad, Boris, but they'll appreciate the opportunity to get even with the FBI; that is, if the price is right. They won't come unless the price is right."

"I pay top money, Lou."

Waiting to hear the double-cross, Lou listens, but knows the way Boris operates.

Boris says, "I got the money. Tell them, a have a suitcase full of hundreds, but they have to take the baby. They can't harm it."

Lou explained how he accidentally met the husband and wife team. Lou was a bank employee in Cleveland. They were cornered, but got away. The bank robberies ended for the two when a retired FBI agent surprised them in Perry.

"I was at the bank in Cleveland when Gorpy and Maud robbed it. They started out in Topeka, Kansas, then robbed a bank in Indiana, Cleveland, and made it to Perry, Ohio. They were sent back to the state pen, in Topeka."

Boris says, "So the FBI did help catch-um?"

Lou says, "Yah, they got lucky. Gorpy can get carried away. He's a mean guy. He might want to rough up the bitch. He doesn't treat women very well. I'm not sure what he'll do to the kid."

Boris says, "You tell him he's not to hurt the kid. No money if he hurts the kid. You tell him that. The lady agent, she burned the organization. We need to teach her a lesson. We'll let him workout his frustration on the bitch."

Lou says, "Maud will take care of the kid."

The call was place to Gorpy and Maud's place. They jumped at the prospect of making fifty thousand. He let them know the terms of the job.

Lou says, "No! You're not going to harm the kid. Just put a scare into her, Gorpy. She won't ever be the same after dealing with you."

Gorpy and Maud arrived after a few phone calls persuaded them that the job was for real. They stayed at a motel. The godfather still had review the job.

Driving to the house, Boris says, "You look like a delivery guy, Lou."

Lou says, "I'm not used to this."

"It's perfect, Lou. Let me tell you one more time. Just after the sun goes down we send in Gorpy and Maud. They take the baby to the convenience store where we switch cars. They take the florist van with the baby and head out of town. It's the perfect kidnapping."

Lou says, "You're nuts."

The florist visit was the next part of the plan, which would be followed by the assault. Boris wanted Lou to handle this operation. He didn't want to take a chance on being seen by the FBI since he already tried to get Monica.

Fairport Harbor was a difficult town to operate in. A newcomer stood out like an American in a Chinese city. Although Boris wasn't parked far away, he wore a wig and fake beard. What worked out well was his use of Lou to check the Micovich house.

The security sign in the window was supposed to worry any potential robber. Getting close to survey inside the house was Lou's job. He was dressed for the part. The florist routine was almost set.

Chapter 18
Paula's Move

It was a God sent idea, the invitation to stay in the guest house which Paula readily accepted. Agent Gavalia temporarily moved into the back house so she could look for another place to live. The timing of the arrangement was perfect just for the fact that Monica's remodeling job was finished and Paula needed a place to stay since her lease was expiring.

While her old Wickliffe condo was close to work and Colby Park offered a convenient place to jog, renewing her lease at her present location meant she would be a good distance from Monica and Michael. Her preference was close friends rather than neighborhood friendships.

Another benefit in the move to Fairport Harbor, Paula would be at the door step of St. Anthony's Church. She liked the small church atmosphere, the choir, and Father Pete.

While Our Lady of Mount Carmel Church and Holy Cross Church were still favorites, she made St. Anthony's the primary church, but she could still visit the other churches on special occasions.

The rustic image was being uprooted in Fairport Harbor. The first big transformations materialize under a mayor and council with unique vision. They invited the Lake County Metro Parks to be caretakers and make the beach a popular attraction.

Generally, Lake County's waterfront was becoming a popular tourist haven. The sensation of a criminal element invading from Canada spawned a mystique which attracted tourists. The incidents along the northern border with Canada after 911 didn't detract tourism. It seemed to create a modern legend. Publicity was positive. Lake County was a land of adventure. Even former residents of Fairport Harbor felt an urge to return.

Paula liked the fact that the harbor town was undergoing a transformation through development. New and refurbished houses, condos, and especially a huge recreation facility were being built near the town. Fairport Harbor's image was changing. It was one of expansion, modernization, and growth. The once sleepy industrial town was experiencing a decided reverse from the days of the smoke-stack industrial era.

Above all, it was more important to be close to her friend especially since the questionable fire or bombing at Mr. Patterson's home was still being determined. The bombing was being construed in several ways. Perhaps he had enemies or was a victim of racial intimidation. Still possible, the model plane simply got away from the owner and he panicked.

The agents had sense not to overreact, but it was very much on the radar screen. The agents were wary about Monica's safety. For now they held back informing Cliff about the connection since he was on vacation in Europe for two weeks. They could wait for him to return.

Keeping a lid on the developing case was their decision. This was a little tactic they learned from agents, Ron Roman and Bill Wright. Those two guys always pulled the wool over Supervisor Moses' eyes or so they thought. Cliff Moses would assign the case if the FBI takes over the investigation. They cherished the freedom to investigate on their own. It was their way of doing business.

Preliminary evidence was still being analyzed at the crime lab. A full report wasn't due back for at least a week because of a backlog.

After Monica and Michael moved back into the remodeled home,

Monica and Paula started to devise a security plan. Together they made a cursory inspection of the repairs. Taking mental notes of the peculiarities of the property, they talked about the layout. Monica gave keys to Paula for both the front and backyard houses.

"Tell me what you think, Paula. Is this place safe? I had Mr. Babb put an additional lock on the doors. He said people never locked the doors when he was growing up in Fairport. But he said that times are changing, so his guys changed the locks to a commercial grade cylinder locking system. I might get a dog when Michael gets older."

With the suggestion of making the house invasion proof Monica invited Paula to inspect the home for security gaps.

The thought of strangers sneaking around seemed remote. A plan was devised by the agents to alert each other by a special cell phone ring. If either woman was in trouble they would sound the cell phone alarm.

Meticulously, walking through the rooms, with her friend Paula at her side, Monica checked the floor boards in the kitchen and hall for the sounds that made creaky noises. Gone were the eerie sounds.

"They're gone, Paula;" said Monica, "The guys did a good job."

All was well until they reached the second to the last step going upstairs. The weight of the baby and Monica on the step set off a minor creak. Paula walked over the same step and couldn't hear anything. Obviously doing some second checking, Paula went over the same step again. No noise was heard.

"You better lose a few pounds, sister. I don't hear anything." said Paula.

Monica says, "Hey, Michael is starting to beef up.

Paula answers, "Blame the baby. Why don't you start jogging with me? I'll help you knock off the baby fat."

Baby fat, I'm not fat. I can still fit into my original clothes."

Paula was leading her along, knowing full well Monica was in excellent shape even after giving birth. In fact Monica was ready to resume martial arts training.

The agents moved to the basement after inspecting the upstairs rooms. Paula was quick to point out the latch on the window over the laundry tub was broken.

"Oh, shoot. I pushed the window shut, but it didn't close all the way. I was going to have that fixed," said Monica.

"Well, most of this place is in good shape. Rome wasn't built in a day, Monica. You can always add a row of nail and broken glass to slow any invaders, says Paula.

"That's a little extreme, girl. I'll put this window on my 'to do' list. For now I'll stick a board over the window.

Chapter 19
Delivery for Ms. Micovich

A van pulled up to Monica's freshly painted colonial. Out jumped a man with a flower box and a card. No one was home at the time. Boldly, the man looked in the front window and went around back to see if anyone was home in the back house. His smartly pressed uniform, shiny black shoes and stately demeanor portrayed a person of responsible character.

Paula answered the door and greeted the middle-aged man. The bright red package and rose red card was held together by a white bow.

"Hello, delivery for Miss Micovich," said the short, pudgy man.

Cautiously, Paula looked to the street to see what vehicle the man was driving. FPS Flowers was on the side of the van.

"Flowers for Miss Micovich," says the smiling man.

"I can accept the package. I'm her friend," said Paula.

The **R. S.**, the initials on the envelope, was a giveaway. Paula's expression, a beaming smile, was immediate. She automatically thought Richard Stern was trying to improve his chances of visiting Monica and Michael. The idea, she thought, was perfect. Mr. Stern was moving in the right direction.

"Sign here, madam."

The man shifted his eyes to the door leading to the basement. It was an old coal bin door. The rusted hinges might make opening the door difficult he thought. Noise was also a factor. Lou made mental notes of what he saw as he returned to his van. As he drove off Boris followed. Behind them, but well down the street was Gorpy and Maud.

When Monica came home, Paula surprised her with the package by ringing her front door bell. She pretended to be the delivery person. Purposely hiding the initials with her hand; she holds out the package.

"Paula, what's this?" asks Monica.

She responds, "Delivery for Miss Micovich."

Both women rushed inside to see what was in the long rectangular box. Long stem red roses came to light as she moved the paper cover off the flowers. The smell was captivating. Monica was reserved at first, but smiled as she read the note. Although the note didn't carry a wordy message, it was fitting.

Welcome to Fairport Harbor, Monica and Michael from a secret admirer.

Paula says, "I'll tell you this much. He's going to try and patch things up, Monica. Mr. Stern is on the right track."

Monica didn't want to show any emotion. The smile was quickly replaced with a cooler sentiment. Opening the door to Mr. Stern would take time. Although deep down she was warming to the idea that he could come by some time in the future. In fact if he was truly trying to resume a friendship, this was definitely a good way to start.

"Don't go jumping to conclusions," Paula.

"I'm not. But I like the smile I saw."

Monica refutes, "No, he isn't winning this easy. Don't think I'm opening the door for him to just waltz in here. Michael and I have to think about this."

Paula finishes with a few encouraging words.

"Well, people do change for the better. I'm sure he wants to see his son grow up. You don't want dad separated from his son. Do you?

Monica answers, "The flowers are nice. We'll see; the question is what's next?"

Chapter 20
Foot Steps

The syndicate's operation in Ohio was under pressure because of the growing possibility that legal gambling was coming to Ohio. Newspapers and the internet carried front page stories about the pros and cons of casino gambling.

For the syndicate legal casino gambling would harm the godfather's operation. The godfather's syndicate already had money-making illegal card games going on in safe houses throughout greater Cleveland, Toledo, and Columbus.

In bars betting on sports games was common practice. The syndicate's bookies were collecting the wagers. Casino gambling would compete with his underground operation, so the godfather didn't want a legal gambling site being built in Lake County unless he had a finger in the operation.

The politicians, mostly in Cleveland and some in Columbus, could've helped him. Unfortunately, Cleveland's politicians were squeamish, having been hurt by Agent Micovich's crime busting investigations. This fear spilled over county borders, eventually making noise in Columbus. In addition her meddling put a scare into less corrupt politicians, the ones who could be bought with large campaign contributions.

With Ohio politicians being less cooperative, it meant the

syndicate would have trouble getting spending bills passed; the ones that enriched the godfather's organization. While the deep seated politicians controlled by the mob still hung with the syndicate, they too were getting antsy. Fortunately, the godfather had a tight grip on these politicians. Chicago and Detroit politicians had the same problem, but Cleveland was important. The godfather's political rope lost some strength in Cleveland after Monica's investigation turned toward some of the county commissioners and their staff.

In the godfather's view no woman was going to decapitate his organization. This was the overriding factor that drove him to order Boris and Lou to get tough with her.

The chauvinistic godfather listened to Boris and Lou's initial plan, but couldn't approve a real kidnapping simply because his daughter had recently given birth to a son and he was ecstatic over the blessing of a grandson. He couldn't order a real kidnapping. However, he could approve some other misfortune, such as, a home invasion or a robbery.

The godfather issues the orders, "Lou, you get Maud to take the child. Maybe it's kidnapping, but we ain't gonna harm the baby. This will really set off the bitch. Then have Gorpy work her over."

Lou wasn't in favor of kidnapping a baby.

"The baby could be misplaced; we don't have to kidnap the baby" says Lou.

The godfather answers "Let me think a minute."

As the godfather pondered the situation, he thought that Maud might need to steal the baby if only for a short time. This would put a major scare into Agent Micovich. A real kidnapping and extortion would bring the FBI out in force. The godfather didn't want that to happen. The idea was kicked around. Finally, the discussion came to a head.

The godfather says, "This robbery must end fast with an ending that achieves our goals. We're going to give the mother agent something to remember, like a bad hair day. She has to experience a nasty evening. We'll use the two assholes."

The instructions to Lou and Boris are specific. Lou is told to hire the losers who are fresh out of prison. Boris is to make certain the perpetrators carry out the job without problems. Agent Micovich's child will be moved to a new location and released unharmed. The godfather didn't want any slip ups. He made it clear.

"Just put a hair-raising scare into Miss Micovich. This job will cure the ambitious ways of an FBI agent."

The godfather commands, "Lou, you know them, go ahead and hire the husband and wife team. Gorpy and his idiot wife, Maud will do. They're out of prison now."

Lou says, "Boss, Gorpy and Maud will be perfect for this job. They need cash. Boris and I already talked about this. Boris can pay them to do this job."

The godfather says, "Good Lou, you guys get it done."

"Boss, Gorpy will be rough. He has a chip on his shoulder after the FBI busted him," says Lou.

The godfather says, "That's why he'll be perfect. Both of them are looking for a job. They need money. You guys work out the details."

Boris asks, "What if something goes wrong, boss?"

"If Gorpy and Maud get busted, oh well, shit happens -- to bad. This job might send them away for a long time. Hey, I'm paying them. We get rid of two losers and the cops think they did a good job of solving a crime. Everyone is happy; that is, well, almost everyone is happy. Ha, ha, ha! "

A smile breaks across the godfather's face. As they watched the boss laugh, all the men joined in a hardy laugh.

The godfather wanted the whole event to be over quickly. The husband and wife team would be sacrificed for the good of the organization. The godfather had reason to eliminate Gorpy and Maud. Always in trouble, the couple caused problems for the syndicate. Heavy drinkers and poor planners put them in prison for armed robbery. They never fit well in the godfather's syndicate. The hired criminals had a rap sheet from Ohio to Kansas. The godfather let Lou and Boris take care of the details. He had no problem with sacrificing two or four little people in his organization.

When Lou called them, the couple jumped at the opportunity to make fifty thousand bucks. A meeting was planned by Lou to meet at a Painesville restaurant to iron out the plans to rob and take Monica's baby. The wheels of the plan seem to come off at some point. Gorpy got confused about the moving of the child.

After going over the plan several times, Lou thought everyone was on the same page. Gorpy and Maud decided the sooner the better. Saturday night was shaping up as the best time to break in and steal the baby. They all agreed, although Lou was skeptical.

Lou didn't like the thought of four newcomers waltzing into a small town. The Fairport Harbor police, he feared, would detect outsiders.

"We'll be out of there in half an hour, Lou. Don't worry, I'll knock the bitch out, tape her up, and Maud will take the baby. Nobody will know. I'm not even going to take my truncheon. I'll leave my calling card on her body. If I have time maybe I'll have some fun with her. Duck tape is all I'll need.

Maud lifted her head to acknowledge the bellicose statements.

Gorpy boasted, "Ya hear that Maud. The agent is going to take care of me."

Maud knew how he could be. She has the final words.

"You'll feel the truncheon, big mouth. You leave the bitch alone."

Over the next two days they got ready. Saturday arrived; they drove around the town looking for a store. A High Street store would serve as the drop off zone.

Some late night activity wouldn't be unusual, so the convenience store parking lot would be perfect.

Gorpy and Maud moved into position. They parked a short distance away near a fruit market. It was almost eleven at night. Seeing a 'house for sale' sign, they walked up the driveway into the backyard which was next to Micovich's backyard house. Stalking eerily in silence, they came to the back door.

Just as Lou explained, the first stage of the robbery, getting into Agent Micovich's place, was correct. At the back of the house was a trap door leading to the basement and a back door. Gorpy also noticed the basement window was ajar on the side of the house. He remembered Lou saying that the back trap door might be the best way to enter.

Gorpy thought he could crawl through the window into the basement, work his way to the back door, and let Maud into the house. He whispers this idea to Maud.

Maud whispers, "Try the back door first, dummy, maybe it won't be locked."

The door was locked and so was the trap door. Turning his attention to the basement window he removed the screen and unfastened the window. He worked his way through, lowering himself to the basement floor.

Using his penlight to point a way to a door leading up the steps to the first floor, he made his way into the kitchen. The back door was only fifteen feet away. Quietly, he unlocked the door.

Maud was ready. She could feel the backdoor handle move. With both robbers inside they found the steps leading upstairs. Looking ahead, Gorpy could see a hallway mini-lamp. It lit up the last few steps.

Creeping slowly up the steps, Gorpy hit a spot on the last step that gave a slight creak. He motions to Maud to be quiet even though it was his fault. The sound travels a second time as he lifts his foot.

Sleeping lightly, Monica heard what she thought was the upstairs step. She opens her eyes and tunes her ears. The baby's monitor was on and she could hear the ceiling fan pushing the air in the baby's room.

A mother's instinct kicked in. She sensed danger; her pulse quickened. Ever so carefully, silently, she reached for her cell phone. She looked at the time on the display. It was eleven thirty-one. Her pistol was in a locked drawer on the other side of the room.

Gorpy motioned to Maud. The baby's room with the door open was off to the left. Waving and pointing to the baby's room, he wanted her to get the child. Revealing the truncheon he had tucked in his waistband, he pointed to himself, indicating he would bludgeon Micovich. Shaking her head in disapproval, she knows his mean spirit. A ruthless man, he is.

Maud moved past him, preparing to snatch the baby. The duct tape on her arm would be used to silence the baby. With the small rubber club in his right hand he darted into the bedroom surprising Monica as she hit speed dial on her cell phone.

His first swing missed as Monica jumped across her bed. She was agile like a cat.

"You know you can't get away bitch. I'm going to have some fun with you," says Gorpy as he leaps on the bed. His second swing moves her into the corner.

Frightened and coiled, she ends the retreat. Like a cat, moving swiftly, she confronts him face to face. Landing a punishing blow square to his face, he backs away momentarily. Angry with blood streaming from his noses, he swings again. Only air is moved by his truncheon. The third miss has him frustrated. Reaching into his waistband to find an equalizer, he momentarily drops his guard.

While the fight raged in the other bedroom, Maud grabs the baby with both hands. She slaps the tape over his mouth and heads down the steps. Hearing Gorpy working to subdue Micovich, she hurries to get out of the house. As she opens the backdoor, she's surprised by Paula Gavalia.

"Stop right there, lady. Who are you? Put the baby down," says Agent Gavalia.

"Stand back, bitch. This is my baby," says Maud.

All of a sudden a crash is heard above them. Glass breaks, a man tumbles across the roof, and falls next to Maud. Gorpy is busted up. Almost lifeless, he lies on his side with blood coming out of his mouth.

Displaying a look of shock, Maud freezes for a moment. Paula rushes at her in an instant burying a thumb in her eye. Screaming in pain, Maud looses her grip on the baby, as Paula snatches little Michael from her.

As an extra measure, she whirls a foot into Maud's throat sending her over the barbeque grill. Landing by the trap doors going to the basement, Maud shook her head almost in disbelief. As she tried to get up, her energy was spent. Maud's head plopped back to the ground.

Monica's fight only lasted a minute and a half. The motherly instinct was foremost as she didn't run for cover. She turned on Gorpy with a vengeance. Responding with a counter attack, her self-defense training came into play. The kick, a frontal assault into the groin caused Gorpy to cry out and inhale. A spasm ran through his body. Holding his privates, lacking muscle control, and bent over at the waist, he wasn't ready for the next horrific kick. Whirling around, she delivered a spinning right foot as he looked up to see a foot greet him. The bare foot sent him crashing through the bedroom window across the back porch roof to the ground below.

Paula yells, "Monica, are you ok?"

Peering out the window, Monica cries, "Paula, the baby, where's Michael?"

Paula says, "I have him. He's ok."

Completely subdued, both nearly unconscious, the criminals were no longer a threat. Paula handed Michael to Monica. Quickly running to her house, Paula grabbed her weapon, handcuffs, cell phone, and identification. On the fly she reported the 911 call with detail.

Paula says, "I'm an FBI agent. We have apprehended a male and female. Send police and a rescue vehicle to..."

Details of the kidnapping, assault, and battery were relayed between two dispatchers. Although Paula was quite upset, she remained calm enough to be specific, so that the first dispatcher could handle the call without difficulty.

Based on Paula's report to the dispatcher, police officers arrived. An assessment of the situation was rendered quickly. Guns were not drawn; officers could see the agents had the two suspects down. Paula gave the officers a quick synopsis of the scene.

The Fairport Harbor police responded first followed by the Lake County Deputy Sheriffs. They merged one after the other.

Paula says, "Officers, we're FBI agents; my partner is in the house."

Just then Monica came out on the back porch. With her hand gun in a holster Monica is prepared to fight. In her other hand she carries a cell phone.

"I guess it's over, Paula. We can let the local police handle these two jerks. I'm leaving a message for Cliff. He needs to know before he asks."

Monica took the ordeal in stride. Although her adrenaline was subsiding, she was clearly ready for more action.

Monica says, "We're alright, Deputy Buckey. We'll have a full report for you as soon as we settle down."

Paula says, "At least this time it isn't Ron and Bill giving Cliff a headache."

Chapter 21
Franco's Casino Team

Palmino Franco was concerned that his bold move to locate a casino in Northeastern Ohio might trigger a negative reaction by some politicians; especially the politicians that have received generous contribution from special interest groups. Illegal gambling organizations, like the godfather's Cleveland syndicate had a free market. Franco was intruding on a cozy operation. In addition casinos located just outside Ohio's borders certainly didn't want competition moving into Ohio. Gamblers from Ohio were dumping money into the area outside of Ohio.

Not intentionally, Franco's identity was becoming a household name in Northern Ohio. He had kicked the hornet's nest. Political friends inside the halls of Columbus would like to take care of the big city politicians.

The big city political apparatus worked overtime to quell the exciting idea of Mr. Franco's sports and gambling park. His projects were just starting, but news was generating generated by the naysayer's. TV ads highlighted the downside of casino gambling.

Big city leaders would love to have a casino in their communities. This would bolster their political fortune. The casino apple was ripening. Competition brings out the best in some and the worst in others. Unfolding was jealousy and envy.

The government leaders that had ties to out lying casinos started to defend their monopoly. Franco saw this jealousy emerge when his casino gained favor in Oregon. He wouldn't back down to temper their mode for he was a competitor. His combination sport's park and casino would be unique.

A sports park, hotel, and casino blended together might seem unimaginable to some folks. Maybe it would be too scary for others. Franco had no doubt the big money people would try to defeat his plan as they did with others. After all, two other casino attempts were defeated by the voters.

To counter this challenge Franco used Brenda Clark as a public relations advisor. She had solid connections to the local government. Her influence would help buttress local support.

Having the Lake County Commissioners on his side would be a necessary first step. After all, they were the political authority. The commissioners could doom his investment. Franco wasn't into politics, but he understood the ramifications. He was sure the commissioners would be on board because of the many jobs that would be created.

The farther along Mr. Franco moved on the project, he became more excited.

"Lake County is an excellent site. The county has a Metro Parks and transportation system, it's all here; it's in place," said the casino owner.

Utility service wasn't a problem. With Lake Erie next to the casino fresh water to support a myriad of activities was certain to attract tourists and sportsmen. The surrounding counties could contribute as well. Manpower, womanpower, and a dozen schools and universities had plenty of muscle and know how.

Brenda Clark would have to cultivate the message. She could explain the advantages to the surrounding community leaders. The school systems would receive huge benefits. By having her as the local mouth piece, she could steady the apprehension.

Lake County citizens would want something more than just a gambling house and this is where Franco planned to shine. Sports would be the centerpiece of his plan. A decent, family orientated, upscale sport's park with a hotel-casino combination to serve the public was the plan in a nutshell. He wasn't just barging in to operate a money-making tourist trap.

The project would be unlike any other casino in America. It would set the stage for future casino projects and likely be the front runner of a modern family vacation. This vacation concept for families wasn't a Disney amusement park, but a sport's park adventure for all ages. Franco would offer free events for small children, sports clinics for older kids, and baseball and softball tournaments for every age group. In addition Franco could tap into local businesses for their help. Golf packages, fishing charters, and water rides would be available to provide variety.

Franco had plenty of ideas and cold weather was his biggest concern. Winter months would be the most difficult time for his operation. The tourism trade would slow. The hotel might have difficulty during the off season. Local ski clubs, cross-country skiing, and indoor sports tournaments besides gambling would have to help support the seasonal change. Special rates for active military and senior citizens during the off season might narrow the budget gap if activity slows down. Trade shows, indoor soccer, racket ball, basketball, and volleyball tournaments would help provide some support. Above all, the casino itself would be an adult only area isolated from family activities.

News of a casino coming to Lake County was leaking out like an iceberg hitting the Titanic. Franco's staff knew plenty, but gossip was twisting in the wind. This news was way ahead of schedule. No ballet issue was even ready. Franco had to marshal his forces to prevent an overly optimistic backlash. Trusting his instincts and wasting no time; he wisely decided to try and deflect the story. As luck would have it, he found a way to massage the coverage.

He sought out professional marketing talent. They would have to come from people who worked in the area. In a most unusual way Franco found who he needed.

The manager of the Great Lakes Mall slipped into the picture when he heard of the casino news broadcasting from a local TV station. The editorial commentary was somewhat balanced between good and evil. Jobs and new money coming into Ohio on one side versus addictive gambling and prostitution on the other hand. These elements were pitched by the editorial host. Killeen Roberts, marketing director of the Great Lakes Mall, also saw the editorial appearing on TV. She told Tony Peskyk, the mall manager, what was taking shape. They both recognize the significance of attracting out of state money and the influx of new jobs to the area.

Killeen comments, "If they're worried about gambling addiction, why do they promote the lottery in every corner of the state?"

Tony says, "Killeen, it's not about mental health problems. Ohio is way behind other states that have casinos. People need jobs. If people are leaving Ohio to gamble in other states then we need an Ohio casino. Ohio's politicians and lottery people are worried they'll lose out to the casinos. They aren't worried about gambling addiction.

"Casino gambling will only come to Lake County if the voters give it the green light. I'd like to meet this gentleman that's building the sports park. Deep pockets and guts are needed to make a venture work."

"There's a buzz in the air, Tony. Keep your fingers crossed. Tourist will pump up the area if the casino idea is true."

Brenda Clark kept Richard as a boyfriend mostly because Stern didn't get in her way. Oh, she liked him. She wasn't looking for marriage, just a companion that she could control. Stern was getting an occasional physical reward for being a close friend.

Mrs. Clark was going to Columbus lobbying the politicians to push for Lake County as a home to an Ohio casino. She'd have Mr. Stern with her as an escort from time to time. Other times, when she was meeting the governor's assistant attorney, she was alone.

As Franco got to know Richard, they became good friends. Along the way Franco told Brenda to try and convince Stern to give up the booze before it consumed him.

One thing about Mrs. Clark, she was a persuasive woman. Stern listened and he did just that, but for other reasons. Stern changed when he gave up the booze. Brenda thought she was brilliant because Stern did as she suggested. In reality Stern wanted his son to grow up seeing a sober father. Monica was another reason, although, ultimately, he started to find his struggle to overcome alcohol would be easier if he turned to God. After a month of sobriety, Stern was offered a position of importance from Mr. Franco. Franco asked Richard to be a public affairs representative for the casino initiative.

Franco said, "Richard, stay off the booze and you could go places in this organization. You know the people, organize, and sell the idea of a sports park. I want you to work with the local kids. You could be a sport's official, become a baseball umpire. Don't stop there, officiate other sports."

Franco's suggestions were important for Stern. He followed up on the ideas. He didn't stop with umpiring. He pursued other roles in sports.

Stern and Franco got along well because of their old high school rivalries. Even though Franco was a rich guy, he liked Stern because he was a regular Joe. He heard of Stern's role with the FBI. Stern was also finding out how difficult it can be to be an umpire and referee in various sports. Their friendship kindled because of their mutual love of sports. Their good natured joust about sports sometimes became the best part of meetings.

Needling Stern, Franco said, "Big brother, Harvey High, always beat the Skippers in football. You remember don't you, Stern?"

"That's bull, Franco Your memory is bad," retorted Stern.

Even in the middle of organizational meetings the two middle-aged men would spar with each other about old times. Although this was a distraction at meetings, Simone Porter would tell Brenda to take a timeout.

"The boys are at it again. Break time, Brenda, let the gentlemen have at it," says Attorney Porter.

Recruiting a marketing team to convince the public a casino would enrich the county was Palmino Franco's challenge. While he found Brenda Clark to be a masterful speaker, good with local politicians, and her personality was magnetic, he knew he needed skilled marketing people on his team. The extra help, the so-called right people, came into focus when Stern and Franco were carrying on a heated discussion about sports.

When the subject of powerhouse schools in Ohio came up, both men agreed, Mentor High Cardinals were the clear winners. At that point both men also realized the City of Mentor was probably the best place to have a rally to focus attention on an issue such as a hotel and casino for Ohio.

Richard Stern says, "Lake County can handle the first Ohio casino. You should advertise this fact in the Great Lakes Mall or have a rally in the Painesville Park."

Franco says, "I want people to know it will be a sports center, a family place, and not exclusively built for gambling. This will be the concept."

"Go to the Great Lakes Mall, Palmino, check it out," said Stern.

The idea stuck in Franco's head. At Stern's suggestion Franco decided to tour the Great Lakes Mall alone as he so often does. He entered the center of the mall where the food court was laid out. As he entered the dining area a female employee at one of the buffet counters offered a free sample of chicken and at another counter he was offered oriental skewered beef. A little farther along a pretty blond about Franco's age offered him another appetizer.

The food court entrance was appealing. Franco thought that he would do the same at his hotel and casino. Offer the public a treat for free, they will come.

He passed a jewelry store and cigar shop as he strolled around. As if he was a mall walker, he blended in with the Great Lakes Mall customers.

He turned back to see where he came from and saw the coffee stand. Pretty girls inside the island in the center of the mall offered a variety of coffee blends. Walking over to the island, Taylor and Rachael served Mr. Franco a dark blend of coffee.

Everywhere he went, Palmino found the mall shops to be staffed by friendly knowledgeable folks. Sticking in his mind, the girls at the coffee island provided him with those teenage smiles. This was the kind of staff he'd have working at the hotel's coffee shop.

Palmino drifted off thinking about the future as he sipped his coffee. Nautical art would adorn one area of the casino and sports memorabilia would be in another wing. Baseball would be his main theme. He thought a casino, if located near the mall, would certainly be an attractive addition to the area. He wasn't that far along with any of the projects. Perhaps a satellite casino in Mentor might work as a high stakes club.

His real desire was to connect kids with sports where kids and parents could be together. Even though gambling was a way to finance some competitive sports programs, tourism and family recreation would be chief benefactor of the casino. This relationship would help support the hotel. If he could blend this atmosphere as the Great Lake Mall has done with shops, it would attract many tourists, sportsmen, and gamblers.

His next stop after trekking through the mall was an informal visit to the mall manager's office where he met Killeen Roberts and Tony Peskyk. Without speaking his exact intentions, Franco said advertising at the mall would make good business sense. Naturally, Tony and Killeen agreed and they had plenty of proof. Franco was impressed with Tony and Killeen's marketing knowledge. He saw the mall as a vision of success. The quick meeting convinced him to use the mall to market his plan. Wide exposure with a diverse crowd would help him win the battle with local voters.

Franco assembled a bigger staff of people moving the meetings from place to place.

One by one he brought on board special people to support his cause. First and foremost he wanted to stay sporty and informal. The third and fourth meetings of his staff were casual affairs, one at Beef O'Brady's in Eastlake and another at Fritz's Restaurant in Fairport Harbor.

Fritz's Restaurant became his backroom semi-private meeting place as Palmino Franco assembled a core group of public relations people. When eloquent furnishings and more seating were needed, they moved down the street to the Honey Hole Club.

They traded ideas. Franco wanted regular folks in the fold that were familiar with the area. At Mrs. Clark's suggestion, a select group of politicians were photographed with Palmino Franco. Lastly, teachers and coaches were added as parts of his marketing campaign. The emphasis was put on art, sports, and family entertainment rather than gambling.

The casino picture in Ohio was starting to appear more often in newspapers. A battle for public support was under way. The lines were drawn. Franco wanted Lake County to be the winner. On the other side it was the big city men with big bucks aligned with big city politicians. The elite power brokers had the deck stacked in their favor. The politicians were controlling the game.

Just by reading the newspaper Franco knew he was up against a formidable group. As his casino plan materialized, he suspected that the opposition would become more ruthless. In his eyes he still had the best idea. A family sports park and casino built next to Lake Erie would attract thousands.

The first question Franco had to answer was a difficult one. Was the opposition forming a loose alliance?

He needed somebody to infiltrate. He already knew about Richard Stern and some of his exploits.

Chapter 22
Brenda's Friend

Since Lake County stood to be a big winner, Brenda Clark was excused from her primary job as department manager to campaign for the casino issue. As the commissioner's paralegal secretary her absence as would be missed.

To fill the void a new department manager was brought in temporarily. Charlotte Galm, a former Fairport Harbor teacher, stepped in to help manage the county's administration department. This sparked a few rumors, especially since the county commissioner's had a few capable people to handle department affairs. Philomena Wheeler was the obvious choice, but she could retire at any time. Another possible candidate was Dorothy Hawkes. She was also leaning on retirement.

Some rumors made sense. Co-workers assumed Brenda's trips to Columbus were two-fold adventures. They wouldn't come out and say it directly. Some thought she might have stepped on the wrong toes and the commissioners were moving her out. Mrs. Wheeler came close to pinning the tail on the donkey when she said that Brenda isn't afraid to go all out to make new friends.

Her close office friends knew she could be a powerful voice. They were whispering that she might leave to run one of Mr. Franco's businesses.

Because Mrs. Clark was the county's best community organizer, Mr. Franco gave her plenty of leeway to help build casino support.

She was asked to spread the word on casino gambling so that Lake County residents could form their own opinion. Even though her position was clear as was the commissioner's position on the casino issue, the commissioners felt it was very important to listen to all parties, both pro and con.

For the most part Brenda Clark stayed focused on delivering an upbeat message. Landing the first Ohio casino in Lake County would create good paying jobs.

Because of Palmino Franco's determination construction was already moving forward on the hotel. He wasn't backing down.

Mrs. Clark knew there would be challenges with Mr. Franco's new venture. It was her role to convince residents and politicians that Lake County was a perfect casino site.

Once a week trips to Columbus kept the ball rolling. Brenda made the trip alone most of the time to lobby the politicians. She left home early and rarely returned from Columbus until the next business day. Although she had more than work in mind, the second boyfriend didn't seem to get in the way. Stern didn't catch on right away.

While the business and pleasure trips were only temporary and had a secretive component, it was important that she stayed focused on the casino issue. The big payoff came after a half-dozen business meetings. She succeeded in convincing a few state officials to support a county casino.

Brenda's promiscuous style wasn't out of character, although she never exhibited this behavior in front of the commissioners. Her charm was captivating to the Columbus lawyer and she knew it. By motivating the young assistant attorney and cultivating favors she did produce political fruit, but it came at a price. Using a combination of tricks, which included late night interludes, she consummated an overly friendly bond.

Forty and looking quite healthy from a crash diet, she usually sported a ruby red dress and matching red lipstick to work the politicos into supporting her position. The lipstick and perfume caught the men's attention like a lint brush.

They attached to her words. It seemed that every appearance she made was greeted with open armed men. She didn't play down her friendliness on the contrary. Using her femininity and convincing discussions, she almost willed the men to grasp important positive positions on the casino issue.

Her political capital grew from every spicy appearance. Seduction being the chief weapon, she extracted from the casino committee a favorable position on the side of casino gambling.

The casino steering committee consisted of three men, who adored Mrs. Clark. Her brunette hair, snug dress, and enchanting words together with her suppleness lessened resistance. Another fact from one member of the committee was a revelation that Mrs. Clark would do almost anything for a political favor. Although not true, she didn't dissuade their thought.

After disarming the casino committee she met with other leaders. In the same manner, but toned down to match the audience, she was brilliant. A charming speaker, she lined up support among the leaders that were hedging on the casino issue.

While she acted somewhat like a black widow spider, her seductive nature did generate a negative side effect. Unknown to Mrs. Clark, she was dealing with Judas. The assistant attorney was a mole working both sides of the street.

Working undercover for the godfather, he relayed some of her revelations. E-mails flowed about the casino plan. On the receiving end was Julius Cambello, the godfather. He paid the assistant attorney a cash reward, knowing that the attorney was a political hawk and member of the Columbus ruling party. As the attorney became trusted, she relinquished more and more information. After a seventh interlude, details of the casino rallies flowed from her lips.

After the romantic quakes, he was temporarily satisfied. In a way he was a captured prey. He wanted more. With each of her visits he became enthralled, enjoying the late night frolics from start to finish. For he too was a man willing to obey and be consumed. He didn't want their passionate meetings to end.

If the godfather found out that he wanted to vote in favor of the Lake County casino, it would be bad. Going against the godfather's wishes, would surly bring the lieutenants to town to settle the score. Dom DeLargo was growing scared.

Richard became convinced that Brenda was having an affair after finding a hotel reservation slip with a man's name on the receipt. Coupled with the fact that she was less eager to have a close relationship with him each time she returned from Columbus, it all added up. When she returned after a seventh trip, Stern confronted her.

"That young attorney in Columbus is certainly spending plenty of time with you isn't he?" Richard asked.

Instinctively, Brenda shot back trying to hide her extra activity.

"What's that supposed to mean?"

"It means you don't get much sleep when you go to Columbus. It's obvious you're worn out from being up all night. Having great sex," snapped Richard.

Brenda didn't want the situation to escalate. Moreover, she wanted to break out of the mutual relationship.

"We're not married."

Richard asks, "Does that mean, well, it's over isn't it?"

Brenda's recourse was to charge Richard with his own promiscuousness.

"I hear you're been busy too. You don't trust me and I feel the same way."

Defending his honor and throwing in the towel Richard resigned and started walking away. Brenda had the last words. She tried to salvage something from the discussion.

"Richard, I worked through the night and have a deal for Lake County. Mr. Franco can proceed with his project knowing the politicians in Columbus are going along with the casino idea. I had to make it happen."

Somewhat hurt and ambivalent, he had something else on his mind to sooth the pain of breaking up.

Richard says, "Hope you can live with yourself."

Stern leaves in a huff.

Not exactly unhappy over their breakup, Richard had someone else on his mind. He was more interested in the lady on New Street, but he could still work with Brenda.

Chapter 23
The First Ohio Casino

The Ohio casino idea floating around Columbus was picking up steam. The trouble with Ohio's economy was widely known. America was in the midst of a recession, so the state's bottom line was red. Something new was needed.

Ohio politicians had already been pressured by the race track owner to allow more gambling. Two casino issues put in front of voters were shot down for one reason or another. If casino gambling was coming to Ohio only a few selected cities could expect the reward. This was the idea at first. The rich entrepreneurs in Columbus, Cleveland, Toledo, and Cincinnati wanted a golden goose to lay an egg in their cities. Another idea was coming into play.

News spread that a successful Oregon casino owner, a Painesville Harvey High School graduate, returned to Lake County with the intension to build a hotel, casino, and sports complex. It was true. One man was moving ahead with plans. The name, Palmino Franco, came up after a junior lawyer informed the governor that a tycoon from Oregon was building in three locations in Lake County. Ground was being excavated. Huge areas could be seen under excavation. A spot near Fairport Harbor by an old factory was being readied. The area could easily encompass many facilities.

At first they were sworn to secrecy; the Lake County Commissioners had a tight lip, but they were making plans for a new enterprise.

Forces of evil marshaled to stop the 'loose cannon' from Oregon. Columbus politicians were starting to be lobbied. News kept surfacing about Franco's project. Entrepreneurs in Columbus, Cleveland, Toledo, and Cincinnati had plenty to say about an outsider coming in to build. Their idea was to make room to them, but bar anyone else from having a casino.

A fight was brewing. The politicians in Columbus were facing a conundrum. Local folks started to rally against the fat cat politicians who wanted to bar Mr. Franco or anyone else from moving in. The politician's seat was starting to sizzle.

Greed and corruption was inching into the picture. As more information flowed, political instigators started to find dirt and create unfriendly waves.

Palmino Franco was way ahead of the curve. He disguised the initial plan. Buying foreclosed property and timely purchases of environmentally molested land gave him a big head start. With the economy in a shambles the properties were offered at fire sale prices. Wheeling and dealing along the way, he bargained for the best price and let people know only a little bit of his plan, but the secret was oozing because of loose lips.

Then he started to build a golf course and baseball fields. Small buildings supported the larger construction. A hotel was taking shape and a casino even though he didn't have every ones blessing. Franco had determination, experience, and wisdom.

Speculation was also surfacing about a change coming to Painesville Township and Fairport Harbor. This change was interesting because of the building going on around the area.

If need be the financial pressure of two schools could be alleviated by merging the systems into one and using the huge tax revenue of a casino to offset the school's money problems. Palmino Franco already had his people tally the numbers and found he could accomplish a perfect marriage if his casino idea is approved by Columbus.

The political machine in Columbus would be his biggest worry.

Mr. Franco was a man of action. He wasn't waiting around for excuses to exclude him from building the first casino in Ohio. Two hotels, a casino, and a large complex were taking shape in two new areas. This was part of his plan. He needed the hotels to accommodate the influx of tourists and game players. His sports complex, another near Fairport Harbor, and still another to the east would feed his hotels. All of these complexes could work to improve the school systems. Palmino wanted to become the first Ohio casino owner who actually had children and family's best interests in his heart.

Chapter 24
Chicago Players Meet

The attempts to get back at the FBI agent were failures. The godfather brought his two underlings back to Chicago. Lou thought that interfering in Agent Micovich's life wasn't worth the hassle. Reluctantly, the godfather decided she was a tough cookie. Boris and Lou totally agreed with the godfather. The idea of screwing with the female agent was put on the shelf. The godfather simply shrugged his shoulders.

The godfather says, "Wasting time on a dame like her isn't worth the trouble. Someday I'll meet her face to face and then we'll see who wins. Right now we have a bigger problem. Somebody is building a casino in Northern Ohio."

Boris asks, "What's the problem, Boss? I like casino gambling. I wish they had a casino in Ohio."

Scolding him, the godfather answers, "Listen, doofus, legal gambling is bad news; this will eat into our own numbers game. If Ohio gets a casino we lose, Boris. But, maybe we can horn in on the building project. We'll get some of our people in there to shake things up."

Lou asks, "What do you want us to do, boss?

"Find out as much as you can about a guy by the name of Palmino Franco. He's rising on the radar screen. The local boys in Cleveland tell me he's moving fast on a building project. Palmino Franco, that sounds Sicilian, so he can't be all that bad."

The godfather had plenty of connections with political friends. The trouble for him was that the politicians weren't about to take the wrong political stand. They were afraid the casino issue was building favorable support.

The godfather says, "My cousin, Sal Cambello, lives in Fairport Harbor, Ohio. Maybe he knows something. Go back to Lake County, Ohio. Painesville is where you're needed, but stay away from the bitch, that FBI agent. She's trouble."

Boris asks, "What do you want us to do, boss?"

"They're planning a casino rally in Painesville. Nose around, you know. Find out what's going on with the casino."

Lou asks, "Are you getting mad, boss?"

"Yes! This woman, Brenda Clark, is the target. I have a friend that says she's been to Columbus to cause trouble for the syndicate. I'm going to send a couple Cleveland boys to resolve the problem. You two verify my next move is done and it won't be pretty," says the godfather.

A plan was needed to stop the developer. Franco was moving too fast. Brenda Clark was on the hit list.

The great fight on New Street was the talk of the town. Inside a little town like Fairport Harbor, this was big news. Two female FBI agents put the boots to a couple of kidnappers which created a swirl of gossip. Everyone in the area fell in love with Monica and Paula. While they wished to be obscure, their actions in a small town made them local heroines.

Their boss, Cliff Moses, found the details of the harbor town arrests on his desk after returning from his European vacation. As he read the first of three reports, one of which was Monica and Paula's account of their ordeal, he hummed a few bars of Indian folk lore music to calm him down. He was kept out of the loop by the agents. The second report sent his blood pressure up a notch. A past experience, in what turned out to be a messy problem, was returning.

Reading the third report, he found that an informer on the street has been saying the syndicate wants to dirty the water in Lake County because of the casino issue. Illegal gambling was a known commodity in Ohio and Lake County had their little card games in various neighborhoods. That was a matter for the local sheriff. It wasn't big enough to warrant FBI attention. However, casino politics were changing the game. A casino feud among entrepreneurs was becoming a controversy.

What blew Moses' mind was one name on the second report. The casino subject contained a watch list with none other than Richard Stern's name in bold print. It took a while to get over the nightmares of Stern's FBI involvement. Seeing his name, Moses could only think the worst. Some Cleveland and Columbus politicians made the list. New names included, Palmino Franco, Brenda Clark, besides Stern. Also flagged was a Cleveland bookie, Fishy Workman and Chicago's, John Paul Beach, alias, the Beaner and Lou Looma. Looma was known as 'the Banker.' Last on the list was Mickie, the Angel, Copko. The angel could count cards. No casino in Vegas would let him play blackjack. These guys were professional gamblers.

Moses remembered Fishy's name. Running a criminal check, he found some information on the man. In Reno Fishy with his wife, Peggy worked both sides of the high stakes tables. His current status was listed as a dealer in Las Vegas while his wife was still listed as living in Reno. Fishy turned informer for the FBI. His record was polished by the Justice Department because he was a protected witness.

Moses' eyes bugged out again when he read Richard Stern was employed by the Royal Flush Casino Corporation. The report read that the syndicate was moving people into the area from Chicago to cause a disturbance at the casino rallies.

Agents Bill Wright and Ron Roman were deployed on two cases so Moses reluctantly picked Paula and Monica to do some surveillance work. With Stern's name out there Moses didn't want Monica somehow tying up with Stern. The job fit Monica and Paula's expertise, so Moses felt ok using his female agents.

After reading the reports, Supervisor Moses allowed them to verbally refresh his mind. Starting from the fire bombing of Doug Patterson's house, the two agents outlined their work.

"Ladies, you're taking a page out of Roman and Wright's detective work. They do their best to hide adventures. Try not to follow their example to the letter. Your story has a happy ending. Gorpy and his wife are headed back to prison. We like happy endings around here."

Paula and Monica were quick to accept Moses' advice.

Moses laid out two packet of information regarding casino rallies.

Moses says, "Information on my desk points to Chicago mobsters coming to Cleveland and Painesville. Seems they don't like Ohio winning a seat in the casino business. Monica, your previous investigations turned up some political shenanigans in Chicago and Cleveland. You upset parts of the syndicate's organization. I believe the bookies are worried about a legal casino coming to Ohio. Politicians and casinos are in the news which leads me to your next assignment. Read about the casino rallies; get out in the field and review the area. See who is showing up at the rallies. The syndicate could be arranging a hit. Take plenty of pictures at the rallies. If it's an evil branch growing, identify it and snip it before it festers."

"We're on it already, boss."

"Good. I'm going to have both of you together, like two sisters, participating at a casino rally. Enjoy Cleveland and Painesville but don't pull a Roman and Wright investigation. I don't like gunfire and I don't want to be the last to know what's happening," said Moses.

Collectively, they walked out of Moses' office. Moses watched as the agents strutted away. He had an uneasy feeling regarding the mafia group. If a godfather was moving people into the Cleveland and Columbus area, trouble was brewing.

Chapter 25
Painesville Rally

R esolute in her actions, Brenda Clark had a single-minded purpose. Determined to make Lake County the stand up tourist attraction in the Midwest, she went about her duty as director of the Painesville casino rally.

Arriving early, Brenda joined up with Richard to mend broken hearts. Succeeding in casual conversation wasn't easy. Richard eventually gave way.

Richard says, "The more I learn about you, Brenda, I can see why you're a leader. You don't let anyone stand in your way."

"Richard, I'm human. I never meant to hurt you. We can still be good friends."

As they were conversing, Richard quickly got over the heartache when he spied Monica Micovich and Paul Gavalia.

The outdoor community event drew residents of all ages. Even Mr. Franco joined the fun as a baseball clown. Parents warmed up to the man who was making the children laugh.

Preferring to remain semi-anonymous, Mr. Franco mingled freely with the crowd. Franco's disguise allowed him to greet folks face to face. This boosted his image, when people realized he was the casino magnet that was responsible for the sport's park being built in Painesville Township.

Mr. Franco insisted that all advertisements be family orientated. Two local banks and the New York Life Insurance Company had advertisements hung on large banners over the main entrance. The family affair included music from local bands. Mrs. Jennifer Kasarko brought art from her company in Fairport Harbor, The Pencil Box Company. She had exhibits under one colorful tent. A short distance away sat the Finnish and Hungarian Museum's tents. They each had a variety of displays to describe the heritage of Lake County through the crafts of early settlers from the 1800's and 1900's.

As the clown made his way through the audience, he was noticed by two well dressed men that weren't there for fun. The suits they wore clashed with the clown suit, but made for an interesting picture that Agent Micovich snapped. As she looked through the lens of the camera, it dawned on her. She saw one of these men in Chicago. She kept silent to see if her partner picked up on the two portly men.

As the event went forward Franco started to notice a pattern and some coolness between Richard and Brenda. Brenda was spending time with a Columbus attorney and Richard was eyeballing two well dressed women. He suspected something was wrong between the two staff members. There was an uncommon coolness separating the two.

Looking like photographers, Agents Micovich and Gavalia continued to mingle among the crowd. Watching and listening, a trademark technique of the FBI, they could read a person's face and tell much about what's on their mind. Profiling, yes, a face and character, gives credence to the sentence 'you're actions speak volumes.'

It didn't take them long to see the unusual. Monica nudged Paula; a wink was all they needed to be sharing the same vibration. Two men stuck out like they didn't belong at the rally. Monica used a wide angle camera to capture a second picture of the crowd. Paying attention to center on the two men, she got decent photographs just as the sun was setting.

Monica was slightly staggered when she caught Richard Stern's image. Richard was looking straight at her. Almost instantly Monica moved into the crowd to avoid his stare. A goofy, girlish feeling rushed into her. She felt good, but didn't say a word to her partner.

Brenda's friend from Columbus was there. Out of the blue Mrs. Clark swooped in on the young man. He moved close to Brenda acting as if they were long time friends. Motioning and pointing behind her back, the idea was to get the mobsters attention. The Judas would have no bounds. If there was any continuity between Dom DeLargo and Brenda, she wasn't in the equation. The attorney was selling his soul.

From the moment Mr. Franco was introduced to Dom DeLargo he didn't like him. Palmino was upset and concerned with Mrs. Clark's abrupt friendship with the junior attorney. It wasn't just a passing acquaintance. Simone Porter noticed the same coziness.

"Maybe she's setting him up to do us a favor Mr. Franco," said Simone.

Keeping the assistant attorney on her side was part of Mrs. Clark's plan. Franco didn't buy it. He had a bad feeling in his heart.

"Is that what they teach wannabe attorneys in law school?" Mr. Franco asks.

"No, but most of the time women know where a man's brain is located."

Brenda Clark felt some guilt because of her continuous actions with the attorney. Richard was doing well. Motivated by the opportunity to see Monica, he didn't want to squander the chance. Unfortunately, time ran out on the festival.

"Let's go have a coffee, Richard. I'll introduce you to a friend from the governor's office. He said he'll meet us at the corner bar. Don't worry, you don't have to drink."

Richard and Brenda arrived first. Adjusting to remove the doubt about their lifestyles, Brenda and Richard attempted to patch up their differences. As the conversation unfolded, her promiscuity was her problem. His drinking was pretty much over.

Somehow the two troubling character flaws that they mutually agreed to curtail became a lightning rod.

Chapter 26
Lightning Strikes Mack's Bar

After they parked the car, Brenda walked on the curbside of the street. Up the street was Mack Crenel's Bar which was certainly a hole in the wall tavern. The South State Street tavern was away from major traffic and situated in a middle class residential neighborhood. The huge parking lot by the railroad tracks ran to the back of the place.

Mr. Crenel was a retired merchant mariner. He worked for Sy 'Smitty' Smith as a caretaker for a Grand River marina. He moved to Parkersburg, West Virginia for a short time, after the marina was bought by the Metro Parks. Mack decided to try his hand in the bar business. Crusty old Mack wasn't one to sit around. Although a miser and naturally, a rich man, he enjoyed adventure.

If Mack had a character flaw, it was his ability to find trouble. Trouble seemed to end up in the hillbilly sailor's lap.

Just before they arrived at the bar, a white Cadillac rounded the corner at a modest rate of speed. Richard looked up and saw the barrel of a gun poking out the window. Before he could speak, the thud of bullets hit the brick building. Richard's shoe went flying as he pushed Brenda behind a parked car. Yelling, Richard screamed for Brenda to get into the bar. Understanding action was needed, Richard grabbed Brenda by the back of the shirt.

They didn't realize the bar was about to close as it was almost ten at night. Mack was about to lock the front door when the two victims burst through the screen door.

"Already had last call folks," said Mack. No sooner did he get the words out of his mouth when a volley of three shots poked holes in the screen above their heads.

Stern yelled, "Hit the deck!"

"What the hell is going on," cried Mack?

Mack grabs Brenda as he starts to understand the gravity of the situation. Brenda is weeping. Her knee is bleeding; not by a gunshot wound, but from the fall outside.

Richard didn't have time to explain. He motions for them to crawl away from the door. Holding Brenda, Mack guides her along.

"Move to the back of the bar," says Stern.

Time seemed like an eternity as they listened to the car roar off. It was only an instant later tires screeched not far down the street. Their ears were like antennas.

Mack calmed down enough to check on Brenda. His chivalry surfaced to help bring a measure of neutrality to the excitement when he spoke. He turned to Brenda with a quip only old Mack could say.

"Your boyfriend is barred for life, lady," said Mack.

Brenda looked at Mack. The tears were flowing as she tries to find the courage to answer Mack. She felt a bit better as she watches Mack act like a medic.

Mack grabbed a bar towel to put over Brenda's wound. Sliding on his butt, Mack moved and reached up to shut off the lights in the place. As he went for the phone, it started to ring.

Everyone felt tortured as the moments passed by. The tension escalated when a car door slammed. The phone was ringing. Mack tried to get to the phone. He wasn't as spry as he used to be. The old man moved to the phone and knocked it off the hook.

With the inside of the bar now darkened, Stern looked up from behind the counter to see the front door. It was still open. Wasting no time he grabbed a bottle of booze to use as a club as he rounded the bar to barricade the door.

As luck would have it, it was a bottle of blackberry brandy he grabbed. Uncaring and shaking, he held the bottle as a weapon. The brandy started to roll down his arm soaking his shirt. Slowly creping around the bar, the tension mounts. Looking ahead Stern takes a huge breath as he rounds the corner of the bar. Oh, so frightening is the shadow appearing in the window.

It moved. Another figure was following. Stern moved closer, but now, less than thirty feet away, the shadows were at the screen door.

Unable to make it to the door Stern darts into a booth. When he looks again, he thinks he sees two figures at the door. A cruel hoax is about to begin.

Voices, he hears voices. The silence is broken when someone speaks. It's the person at the screen door.

"Painesville police, is everything OK?"

"Hell no, we need help!" Stern yelled.

Nervous, but somewhat relieved, Stern popped up his head for a moment. At the same time he could hear Mack. Ducking back down and listening, he makes the sign of the cross. Stern's chest is heaving from the fright and flight.

Time stands still as his senses detect the change in the air. The smell of blackberry brandy permeates the room. Something is wrong. Stern tries to speak, but the words wouldn't announce his worry.

Mack answers the phone in a frantic voice.

Mack shouts, "Hello, police, we need help!"

An echo seemed to be floating in the room.

The voice on the phone asks again, "Painesville police - is everyone OK?"

Mack says, "Just get over here, we need help!"

The man at the door speaking on the cell phone boldly asks. "Who's in there with you?"

Mack says, "Two people, a man and a woman."

Stern finally pulls himself together and whispers, but projects in a deep voice to Mack.

"Hey, no, no, he's at the door! It's not the police."

The man on the phone says, "Stand up and come out with your hands up. We want to see you." Mack thought for a second and then hangs up the phone. A sick feeling swept through him as he heard the squeak of the screen door.

Stern's level of anxiety intensifies as he realizes the reality. No flashing lights or sirens were flashing or echoing. The only lights on were nightlights as Stern's eyes start to adjust. Wide eyes scan toward the door as he peeks. The shadows that were at the door; they vanished. Stern moved cautiously trying to make his way to the door when a man surprised him. In one hand was a black pistol with a silver silencer screwed into the nose of the gun. The reflecting image on the wall was that of two men.

"Surprise!" said the dark suited man.

"Have a drink, mister." The man was dialing on his cell phone. The bar phone started to ring again.

Almost instantly, Stern put the blackberry bottle to his mouth. He listened to the man speak into his cell phone.

"This is the Painesville police, is everything OK?"

Stern could hear Mack speaking.

"Hell no! Where are you guys. We need help right now!" Mack yelled.

Stern gulped down a couple more ounces as he started to figure out they were in big trouble. A thought flashed in his mind about Monica and his son. Appearing behind the first man was another gunman. The first mobster moves to see who is talking behind the bar.

The second man says, "Let's finish it. We gotta go!"

Exceedingly desperate, Stern raised the bottle as a weapon. The blackberry brandy was flowing down his arm.

Holding the gun over the bar, he was about to execute Brenda and Mack. Mack grabbed Brenda to shield her.

"FBI, cried the woman,"

The winging rear doors flew open as Agent Monica held her arms out with pistol in hand. The assassin hanging over the bar spins and turns his weapon toward Monica.

Stern flings the bottle of brandy at the men at the same time shots ring out in the bar. Crashing glass and bullets fly through the air. As full scale panic sets in, Brenda screams. Then it's followed by seconds of silence. Crying behind the bar is Brenda. Mack holds her tight. A mere second passes as a body hits the floor close to Stern. The second mobster falls next to him.

With weapon in hand Agent Paul Gavalia races behind the bar to check on Brenda and Mack as Monica slowly walks over to the lifeless criminals. She holds her handgun rigidly fixed on the hit men.

As Monica passes Richard, she accesses the scene and coolly asks a question.

"Richard, are you OK?"

Quite relieved, Richard replies, "Monica, what can I say."

Monica asks, "Are you OK!"

"Yes, thank God."

The scary ordeal was over. Down the road sirens blared. The wailing sound was getting closer as the Painesville police and Lake County Sheriff's cars approached the scene.

"Richard, your son wants to see you someday."

With that statement Monica helps him off floor as Stern wipes his face.

Richard says, "I was sober, Monica."

Monica says, "I want to believe you. Michael wants to see a decent father."

Almost crying, Richard says, "Monica, I'm sorry. I can be a decent dad."

Agent Gavalia was on the cell phone explaining details of the crime scene to the dispatcher. She watched Monica and Richard converse for a moment. In her heart she thought he might have a chance with her. She knew Monica really wanted him.

She wondered. Maybe Monica just wanted a father figure like her dad. Monica's father was just as adventurous as Stern, but was he as careless and brazen?

Agent Paula wanted to tone down the situation. Walking towards Monica and Richard, she says, "Mr. Stern, you need to find new friends. I told you, stay out of the bars."

Stern asks, "How did you know we were here?"

Paula answers, "We examined the photographs of these goons. Monica positively identified one as being an associate of the Chicago mob. That was enough for us. We followed them to their car and tracked them using a planted GPS device. The GPS malfunctioned for about five minutes and we lost them. Then it started working again."

Monica says, "Agent Roman let us use the GPS tracker. It's not supposed to go out like it did. You're pretty lucky. Michael almost lost his real Dad."

Richard was overjoyed she said that. He says, "I want to see him, Monica. I want to teach him baseball. Dear God I want to hold my son."

Monica says, "Dad, just stay off the booze. You can teach him how to play baseball. Don't you worry?"

Richard says, "I'll buy him a baseball glove and a bat."

Paula adds, "You better wait a couple years on the glove, Mr. Stern. Michael has to crawl before to can get to the pitchers mount."

As the police arrived everyone came together. They all felt relief and hugged each other. Paula couldn't contain her happiness.

Within a minute the ambulance siren was echoing outside.

Paula says, "Let's get you folks to the hospital."

Mack winks at Monica and flashes the OK sign at Paula. Richard smiles broadly as he passes the Painesville police and deputy sheriffs.

Love and violence meet at Mack Crenel's bar.

Book 4
Chapter 27
Monica's Dream

Mack's tavern was still crowded two weeks after the shooting. Customers chatted and argued about the crime scene. Back and forth the gossip flowed. The people living on South State Street worried for a month until the gossiping died down.

Supervisor Moses was satisfied with the report from his two brave agents. The outcome of a very dangerous situation could have been awful. He wasted no time explaining the benefits of heading off trouble.

Moses says, "We need to separate the criminals from the peaceful and tranquil citizens. This job got very messy. Now don't get me wrong, I understand the rules of deadly force."

Monica says, "It happened so fast, boss. We didn't have time to say boo."

He told Agents Micovich and Gavalia to trade in the impersonation of Agents Bill Wright and Ron Roman for a less dramatic conclusion.

Moses says, "Well, both of you have been asked to attend a ceremony in your honor."

He explained the details and let them know he would be there to celebrate with them.

Cliff says, "Agents, please keep your words to a minimum. Let me do most of the talking at this function because we'll need to make our presence known, but not go overboard. I have a feeling we'll be seeing more activity in Lake County. The people in Ohio just might vote for casinos this time around. That's going to bring a ton of money into Ohio."

Sensing the supervisor was hitting on a point, Paula lets him know they understand.

Paula says, "Don't worry, boss, we're not looking for the limelight."

Officials from Lake County, Painesville Township, the City of Painesville and the Village of Fairport Harbor gave tribute to the new harbor town residents and local heroines. By throwing a party in their honor, they called attention to the FBI's crime-fighting ability. At the celebration government dignitaries included Fairport Mayor Reese Conway, Commissioner Ray Sines, and Painesville Township Trustee Jim Falvey. One by one they each spoke a few words of congratulation. Near the end of festivities Commissioner Sines called on Painesville Township Engineer Ted Galuschik to outline recent developments in the county. This provided an opportunity for smooth talking Mr. Galuschik to speak about new construction projects.

Naturally, the new sports park was highlighted along with the hotel, but the casino issue was very much on the mind of everyone present. References to the casino were guardedly spoken, so as to not cause a controversy. The power brokers in Columbus were protecting the big cities and black balling Franco. Still, the entire Franco project was high on the list of structures being built in Painesville Township.

Knowing the township had a shot at being the first Ohio hotel and casino to open, he played down the big city intrigue. Finally, Ted called upon Agent Micovich and Gavalia to offer their words. The applause was loud. Graciously, they turned over the microphone to let FBI Supervisor Cliff Moses offer his words.

Moses was well prepared to talk about the FBI. He thanked the lady agents and stepped to the podium. With a couple quick humorous lines, Moses remarked that citizens can be proud of the service all law officers do everyday.

Moses handled the spokesperson role with ease. He provided insight about the history of the FBI and the rigors of the job. Moses spoke of the founding in 1908 under President Theodore Roosevelt. J Edgar Hoover was the director who shaped the FBI. In the early days the agency assisted the Treasury Department with its special agents.

Moses was the perfect counterweight for his agents. The ladies were humbled by his speech. Throughout the evening the ladies tried to play down the heroine role. They didn't want to be honored for doing their duty.

In order to tone down any reference to organized crime and casino gambling Moses told attendees a known fact. Casinos and banks have something in common. They attract law abiding citizens as well as less savory characters. Moses said it was part of the FBI's business to respond and stay on top of crime when they detect lawbreakers.

The party broke up and nearly everyone went the own ways. Out in the parking lot Moses let the ladies know he was proud of them. He had another step for them to follow.

His idea was to give the agents some time off. This time was a form of rest and relaxations to diffuse the after effects of a job well done. His suggestion was to get away for a couple weeks.

Moses instructed the women to tone down their affairs. With Paula standing next to Monica, Cliff explained a concern he had.

The supervisor says, "I need to examine the dynamics of the case. From the beginning with the fire bombing in Willowick it appeared that organized criminals are people we need to watch. Now this shooting happens. I'm starting to see the big picture. The casino business is heating up in Ohio."

After pulling out pictures from his brief case he continues.

"These photographs indicate plenty. The pictures you took at the casino rally, they're proving a point. They're pointing at underworld figures. The mob is getting antsy."

With all of this on going on the supervisor adds another fact. Cliff's head was ready to explode because of the old face rearing his head. Anytime Richard Stern is involved and he is in the picture, Moses expects trouble.

He didn't want to tell the agents that he is bringing in his best investigators, Roman and Wright to review the shooting. He wanted agents protecting agents by looking over the entire case. Any new detail found might provide the link to the crime boss.

"For now you and Paula use the next fifteen days of paid leave to see America. There's so much to see. The FBI wants fresh, relaxed agents. You're going to be keyed up a bit right now. Here's two tickets to fly anywhere in the United States."

The paid leave was almost shocking, but not totally out of line. Moses had reason to believe that the lady agents were taking chances and getting off course.

The lady agents respond, "Thanks, Cliff, we'll make good use of the tickets."

Cliff spoke with a measure of urgency. He wanted the agents to get away for the time being. Knowing Cliff Moses wasn't being generous, they'd follow through with his suggestion.

Paula and Monica knew an investigation would follow up on their report. Monica wasn't on the job that long after delivering the baby, but she wasn't complaining. Paula always wanted to go to Hawaii. Although they didn't expect special treatment, they weren't going to say no to free airline tickets.

Moses hopped in his car and waved at the agents as he drove off. They could hear him humming an Indian folksong as he passed. If Cliff was singing that usually meant he was feeling some stress. Moses detected the strain of the job. An FBI agent can suffer fatigue and that's why he suggested a vacation.

Paula asks, "Poor Cliff, he's got a lot on his mind. Monica, is there a better place to recuperate? I mean; why can't we go to Hawaii?"

Traveling to Hawaii was the perfect way to get away from the upheaval. The time off gave them an opportunity to see the island paradise. The vacation did act as a relief valve. Although Michael was too young to enjoy Waikiki Beach, the agents found the sun and surf to be a heavenly experience. Unfortunately, it wouldn't last.

The trip had an overshadowing event. A late night dream would tell of things to come.

On the third night of their stay Monica had a haunting dream. Paula woke to find her partner calling out in the dark. After listening to Monica mutter for a minute, she could barely understand the action. It was something about Richard. When Paula came to her side to wake her, she distinctly heard words referring to Monica's past.

Monica says, "Richard, get in the car!"

As she shakes her, Paula says, "Monica, hey, Monica!"

Monica replies, "Richard!"

Paula says, "Monica, wake up. It's me."

Monica was embarrassed by the nightmare. She apologized. Paula didn't say much after Monica was fully awake. She just told her partner to relax.

Paula says, "I have weird dreams too."

Flying back to the states on the last part of their trip was a little sad.

With only a couple days left they traveled back to Ohio. They unpacked and prepared to rejoin the crime-fighting operation.

Jet lag contributed to a restless night for Monica over the weekend.

Monica dreams.

They were at Mack Crenel's tavern in Painesville.

The lifelike vision of her shooting the mobster before he could execute Brenda Clark subconsciously popped into her mind. Partially awake almost in a trance, she rose on her elbow and felt the pajama top. It was damp from perspiring.

The ceiling fan swirled above the bed as she sunk back under the covers.

It was still very early in the morning. Forcing her memory to recall the dream, she could see *Richard lying on the tavern floor. Was he ok?* Thankfully, *he moved.* A relief wave rushed through her body.

Hearing Michael, Monica got up to check on him. She wondered if the dreams carried a hidden message. After picking Michael up, she thought, maybe she should go see Richard and make sure he's OK.

End Part One

Looking Forward
Part Two

Monica wanted to check on Mr. Stern just for the simple reason that her dreams were pointing her in that direction. She told Paula she had the dream again.

Richard Stern is preparing for a new role. He has a new position of leadership.

How many casinos would be operating in Ohio? That was a question for the state legislature. Only four licenses were approved. Franco wanted to know, why? He asked the question. Why not in Lake County? The answer was simple. Power brokers wanted total control of Ohio gambling. Only the big cities could have casino gambling. Franco wasn't about to be shutout.

A hotel, casino, and tournament baseball are about to change Stern's lifestyle.

The godfather isn't through. This was the concern of Cliff Moses. Moses knew the mafia was looking to worm their way into Ohio's casinos. A power struggle was brewing among the big cities, the syndicate, and the state lottery. Everyone wanted a piece of the casino pie. Money was corrupting the system. Greed was the reason.

Moses interviews two new agents. Added to his force were Agents Kayla Jacobson and Nicole Swider. They would be part of the task force keeping an eye on the syndicate.

Skipper

Agents Roman and Wright review the work Monica and Paula have done. In many ways they can reflect back on their past and see the mistakes. Rather than tell Cliff Moses about some idiosyncrasies they protect Monica and Paula.

Someone is revealed who is trying to stop the Lake County casino from being a reality. This prominent person has a tie to Columbus and the syndicate. Roman and Wright find out by way of Stern. The going is tough as they get close to the top tier in government. Events impacted their lives in a dangerous way. As usual Richard Stern manages to be in the same area as the FBI agents.

Palmino Franco, the one person that had no ties to politicians or the underworld, who should be operating a casino, is being railroaded. Big city business men are behind the plot. They don't want competition. Franco knows the depth of greed. He faces off with Goliath.

Introduced in Northern Ohio is a brand new way of intermixing tournament play with entertainment. Franco's game brings a new form of casino gambling to Ohio. He's behind tournament sports in Ohio. He has a unique approach to sports.

His sport's parks are built one after another. The big city politicians are lobbied to shutdown this offensive tiger. Jealousy fuels the body of city businessmen. The horns of greed are illuminated. Franco must stay calm under the mean spirited on slot.

His ballparks are made for children. Franco understood the balance a family needs when traveling on vacation. Beauty on a grand scale is the terms to describe the things he has done. The grand opening celebration of the Victory II Hotel and Casino is a sign of hope. Successfully launch, Victory 1 and the Royal Flush Hotel and Casino are other places that Mr. Franco has opened.

Monica Micovich finds out that her son, Michael, and his friends have an idol. It's her. She has the special qualities most moms carry. Although the mini-detective service the children invent is a replica of her FBI character, she makes light of the children's ingenuity. She didn't realize how far the group would go. Even Cliff Moses is impressed.

Coaches are always looking for new talent. The new boy in town is Jonathan May. Michael teams with his friend, Jonathan and a host of other classmates to write a new history in Fairport Harbor sports. It's not just to play baseball. The New Street organization of boy and girls are incorrectly labeled. A gang of kids is not a street gang. They operate various enterprises. The youthful detectives look to their leaders for guidance. This has Richard, Monica, and Paula Gavalia back on their heels. The adolescent crime-fighting force must be tempered.

Along comes Skipper, a dog, who arrives in a most unusual way. This isn't just an ordinary mixed breed. He interacts with the baseball team.

Richard Stern shed some of the problems. New ones seem to surface. In his past was the answer to all of his problems. In order to improve the future he has to ask Him to light the way. Stern didn't get it. The message was repeated many times by Father Pete.

Not all conditions were improving after Stern got off the booze. For each step forward he found a new hole to get stuck in. He found it difficult to stay on the right path.

With Stern's ability to make predictions people started to ask him in advance about the outcome of games. Stern had a reply. Casually answering the question he says, "I'm studying entropy."

Word got back to the godfather that a man was correctly predicting the outcome to football games. When the godfather found out that Stern was an umpire, he sent his lieutenants out on a recruiting mission. The godfather thought about the information. This could be a golden opportunity. Was he really that psychic? Then it dawned on him.

The godfather says, "This guy is rigging games. We need him."

In addition the godfather heard about his other exploits. The running battle with terrorists, his work as an amateur bounty hunter, and he found out Stern was once an informer for the FBI. His work history seemed unreal.

The godfather says, "This guy is like a Captain on a ship. He goes from one adventure to the next.

The evil people definitely wanted Stern's help. They could use a man with this talent to enrich themselves. They were willing to buy a prediction.

The uncertainty of the casino outcome was something Franco had on his mind. The investment was enormous. His casino plans faced challenges from the mafia. They wanted a piece of the action. When the politicians got involved, this made matter even worse. Even Franco was looking to Stern for a prediction.

Competitions in life come in all sizes. Games are being played by good and bad people. The right outcome is tough to reach. Each character builds a fortress. Either they're protecting their money or defending their honor. Franco preferred to be the attacker. He wasn't standing idle while others came to reap the rewards.

The casino issue was only one aspect that was changing life in Lake County. Identifying those bad guys, the individuals and groups was the FBI's job. Cliff Moses had a crew of agents to handle that daunting task.

The casino, a women, children, and youth baseball present challenges for Richard Stern. Mom, the FBI agent and the kids make life very interesting.

Suspense is nothing new for Monica and Richard.

Monica must resist getting involved with conniving spectators. One man in particular keeps showing up at her son's tournament baseball games.

The godfather's daughter has a son the same age as Monica's son. The godfather's grandson has pitched against the Skippers. Michael's team and the Chicago team will be meeting again on the baseball field.

Although she had held her temper and watched her son perform admirably in the past, the next contest is huge. More is at stake in this game for the godfather has a score to settle with the FBI agent.

Stern sat in the bleachers begging to see into the future. He wondered if all the lessons he taught his son would be enough.

Young Michael Micovich is growing up and learning how to be a leader. Michael is a Skipper.